HEY CHICKEN MAN

Susan Brown

Cover by David Craig

Scholastic Canada Ltd.

Scholastic Canada Ltd.
123 Newkirk Road, Richmond Hill, Ontario, Canada L4C 3G5

Scholastic Inc.
730 Broadway, New York, NY 10003, USA

Ashton Scholastic Limited
Private Bag 1, Penrose, Auckland, New Zealand

Ashton Scholastic Pty Limited
PO Box 579, Gosford, NSW 2250, Australia

Scholastic Publications Ltd.
Holly Walk, Leamington Spa, Warwickshire CV32 4LS, England

Canadian Cataloguing in Publication Data

Brown, Susan
    Hey chicken man

Originally published as : The black tunnel.
ISBN 0-590-71611-5

I. Title. II. Title: The black tunnel.

PS8553.R6886H49 1991   jC813'.54   C91-093365-0
PZ7.B76He 1991

9 8 7 6 5 4   Printed in Canada   1 2 3 4 5/9
                       Manufactured by Webcom Limited

Contents

1
Chicken Man!

Tom Kirby was chicken and everybody knew it. Billy MacPherson had made sure of that.

From where he lay in the shade of one of the cherry trees, Tom could see Billy and the others strung out in a dusty line of bicycles on the side road that bounded the orchard. Probably Billy had decided that the gang should head towards the conservation area for a swim.

Tom's stomach seized up. He wanted to disappear, to sink deeply into the shorn grass of his family's orchard before the boys got close enough to see him. But he was too proud to move.

Billy had almost passed by before he noticed Tom lying motionless in the shade of the small tree. Their eyes met for an instant; then Billy wheeled his bicycle around and stared with raised eyebrows.

"Well!" he said in mock surprise as the others pulled up around him. "Look who we have here!"

"Chicken Man!" Skinner drawled in his high, nasal voice.

Tom was used to this, but he winced inwardly when Chris, Joey and Mike chanted in much practised unison, "Buck-cluck-cluck!" He stared into the distance with as little expression on his face as he could manage while they roared and snickered.

"Well, c'mon, Cobras," Billy said with exaggerated contempt. "We have better things to do than cackle with Chicken Man."

The others snickered again and rode off down the road shouting "See ya, Chicky!" and "Look out for the Cobras!" behind them.

Tom lay unmoving until he was sure they were out of sight. Then he jumped up and threw down the grass stem he had been chewing. He stared in the direction they had gone and clenched his fists. For a moment he thought how good it would feel to smash Billy MacPherson a good one right in his fat, leering face. But that wouldn't help. The others would still yell "Chicken!" at him when they knew they were out of range.

Tom strode off towards the other side of the orchard. He yanked his bike out of the shed and set off down the lane and onto the gravel side road. He paused for a minute and thought of going to swim at the conservation area despite Billy, then decided against it. There was no point in asking for punishment.

They'd never jump him, of course. Billy was a bully, not a fool. They'd tried that once last fall, but Tom had just fought it out as best he could, landing a few good punches and taking about three dozen. But the next day he had waited till he could get Billy by himself and had blacked his eye and given him a nosebleed. For all his size and bullying, Billy was no fighter without the others to back him up.

As the tires of Tom's bicycle scrunched over the gravel, the dry dust of the side road billowed around him. He pumped hard up the curved, steep hill that led into town. After the first fifteen metres the hill was less steep, but it continued with a slight incline for about one and a half kilometres until it reached the town. Then there was a sharp curve and another steep section as the road snaked up the side of the Niagara Escarpment.

Tom was perspiring heavily and his face was streaked with dust by the time he reached town. He thought of riding to MacDonald's Pharmacy for a coke, then changed his mind. He didn't feel like seeing anyone this morning. With a sudden fierce need to get entirely away from people, he began the hard ride up the road leading to the top of the Escarpment. He managed to pedal about seventy-five metres up the steep road past town before he had to get off and walk. It gave him a sense of satisfaction.

At the top of the road Tom stopped to rest at the gravel turn-off the government had built for sightseers. He loved this view more than any other in the area.

Leaning on his bicycle, he could survey almost every bit of the countryside he knew so well. There at his feet was the Escarpment, covered with brush and trees and patches of bare rock where the incline was too sharp for even the tough bushes to find a secure hold. In front lay the prairie-like flatness of — what? A valley maybe? But there were no hills on the other side, just the glittering blue expanse of Lake Ontario stretching to the horizon.

Tom often wondered what had made the land so flat. He felt as though he could almost reach out and run his hand over the rich textures of the countryside, like some huge possessive giant: the patches of green orchards like mossy velvet, the vineyards like a spiky, ordered terracing of grass, the buildings like hard, scattered building blocks, and the Queen Elizabeth Way, stretching south and east to Niagara Falls, like a ribbon of hard glue, sun-dried in a random pattern.

From where he stood he could see a familiar cluster of houses. His own home stood out, bright white and sprawling, with its pinkish, pointed and partly gabled roof. His parents had bought it because it was so old — almost a hundred and fifty years. Surrounding it were the two small orchards, one of cherries, the other of peaches. The white shed that served as catchall and garage was actually an old carriage house from before the days of cars.

The other houses seemed more naked than his own because they were new bungalows, unscreened by trees, less belonging to the area. Just over a year ago Billy MacPherson's parents had bought the big, showy one at the far end.

Tom's teeth clenched as he thought of Billy again. If it hadn't been for Billy, no one would ever have thought of the initiation and he would still be the one who decided things, instead of Billy. No one but Billy could have found Tom's own private weakness, the one he'd never told anyone. Until Billy came along it had just been a rough edge on the back of his mind, something that grated sometimes but was usually easy to avoid and forget.

Suddenly Tom turned his back on the view. Well, he'd show them. He'd go finish the initiation now. There was no time limit. He'd do it right now.

With cold determination, he pushed off on his bicycle. As he pedalled, Tom made plans about how he would casually flaunt the pocket knife he would retrieve. He wouldn't come running up to Billy and the others the way Skinner had, shouting, "Look, I did it! I'm part of the gang now too, aren't I?"

No, Skinner was two years younger, and that was the way a little kid would do it. Tom would carry the knife in his back pocket, with maybe a small piece of wood. The next time Billy and the Cobras started to call him

Chicken Man, he'd casually take the knife out and start to whittle. It would be rusty now from lying in the water for almost ten months, but the rust would just add to the effect.

Tom gloated over his image of Billy's reaction. It would be worth all the humiliation of the past year to make a public fool out of Billy.

He forced his mind to dwell on the scene. If he allowed himself to think of what he had to do first, his stomach would seize up as it had so many other times, and the thought of the Black Tunnel would fill him with a terrible fear. No, he would just think of how he'd make a fool of Billy. I have to do it this time, he thought desperately. This time has to be different.

After a kilometre of furious pedalling, Tom was panting from the exertion. It was a long way. The trees had thinned, and for the rest of the way the road was exposed to the hot sun. The pavement ahead looked rippled, distorted by the rising heat waves.

Tom felt calmer now. At least if he didn't make it this time no one would know the difference. He would pretend he thought the whole thing was kid stuff, and that he had no intention of ever trying it. They didn't have to know about all the Saturdays and holidays he had spent up here. Once he had even come in winter, though he had nearly killed himself climbing down the icy cliff.

If they didn't know, then things couldn't get any worse except in his own mind, Tom thought gloomily. Even his parents had started talking about his lack of confidence, his slipping grades and his anti-social behaviour. They didn't know the truth because it wasn't the kind of thing that parents understand. They thought he didn't want to hang around with the other kids, or play hockey, or anything. How could they know that the other kids would have nothing to do with him?

Tom continued slowly. Occasionally a car passed him, full of tourists taking the scenic route along the top of the Escarpment. This road was pretty but the one at the foot of the Escarpment was faster; so there weren't too many cars to spoil the quiet isolation of the morning.

Finally Tom came to the old mill and stopped. It was now a museum, managed by the man whose great-grandfather had built the mill. Mr. Piers couldn't stand kids hanging around. Tom thought it was really funny how the old man would hover over the kids as though he were afraid they would break things. How could anyone break the insides of a mill made of wooden beams and iron? Or better still, how could anyone break a water-fall? Old Mr. Piers had even fenced that off.

Tom saw Mr. Piers poking around the grounds, pulling up the odd weed and nervously watching two boys who were innocently fishing in the widened river below the falls. He chuckled at the thought of the old man's frantic worry about what they might do.

Mr. Piers knew everything about the river that had once run the mill. He even made it his business to know what the people at the nearby waterworks plant were doing, because the runoff from the reservoir that supplied St. Catharines with water was occasionally released through man-made tunnels into the river's gorge.

There was a whole series of runoff tunnels in the Escarpment, Mr. Piers had once told Tom. They were interconnected, and some were several kilometres long, drilled through the solid, sweating limestone of the Escarpment. The Black Tunnel was one of these.

Tom got back on his bicycle and pedalled slowly down the road. When he was sure Mr. Piers wasn't watching, he swiftly turned into the rutted lane that led down behind the mill, past an abandoned farm house, into an overgrown field, and to the path that would take him down into the gorge.

He hid his bike in the bushes and began the difficult climb. Unless you looked carefully, the first section seemed impossibly steep, until the cliff finally jumbled itself into a half-overgrown hill that angled down to the river. But if you knew where to look and how to climb, here and there you could find a bit of rock where you could wedge your feet or find a handhold. There was one two-metre drop with no handholds. But at the side of it a wild grape vine had spilled over the top of the cliff and sent its roots and seedlings into little cracks and crevices in the face of the rock until vines coated half the cliff face. The main vine, if you groped for it among all the leaves and tendrils of its offshoots, was about half as thick as a man's wrist. The boys had tested it three summers before and it had held the weight of five of them without budging.

Carefully Tom slid down on the seat of his jeans, until the cliff was too steep to go any farther that way. Then with a practised movement he twisted over, hanging for support to a handy piece of tree root that looped out of the rock before turning back into the bit of dirt again. His feet scrabbled for a hold and finally found an outcropping that would hold him. His other foot he wedged against a platform covered with sticky mud.

Carefully testing each foothold and handhold to see if it would bear his weight, Tom climbed down to where the cliff became too sheer to find any hold at all. Then he groped until he found the father vine. Once he had it grasped firmly in both hands, he pushed his feet free and with a Tarzan yell swung himself down the rest of the way. That was the best part of the climb. The scrapes and bruises were just the scars of a successful battle with the cliff.

Tom jumped and bounded the rest of the way down to the edge of the river. For a while he stood quietly in the complete isolation of the gorge. It was full of sounds — water sounds, bird sounds, wind sounds, even chipmunk, squirrel and other small animal sounds — but it seemed wonderfully still, because there were no people or machine noises.

With a surge of his old confidence, Tom walked slowly along the riverbank towards the roar of the waterfall. He hopped over rivulets that trickled from the sweating cliff into the river and jumped onto the cushioning softness of logs that had lain moist and unmoving for years, slowly rotting back into the ground.

He always felt that this was his own place, made especially for him. Adults never came here. The beauty of the gorge and the stream, with its progressively smaller waterfalls, was not enough to bring them clambering down the rough cliff. The tunnels that fed into the gorge had been blasted and mined out almost fifty years earlier.

There were two tunnels opening into the gorge. The smaller was high in the sheer cliff — a scar drilled into the middle of the face of the Escarpment rock. It was impossible to climb to.

Farther up the gorge the second tunnel was cut into the cliff beside the cool, bowl-shaped basin of the waterfall. A steep hill of loose rock and shale, refuse from when the tunnels had been drilled, spilled from the tunnel mouth, making it easy to reach.

There were few traces that the tunnels were not natural — only the rusted rails for the cars which had carried out the rock, and the remains of a metal grille which had once been fastened over the entrance of the second tunnel to keep people and maybe animals out of the drainage system. The grille had long ago been wrenched off, and now it lay with the rails in the water which covered the bottom of the tunnel.

Tom stared at the smaller tunnel. Directly in front of it was a semi-circular ledge about a metre wide, which narrowed down to nothing at either side of the tunnel. The spill-off of water had gouged a small pool in the ledge. Tom could see the rippling reflections of the water on the rock above the tunnel mouth. His pocket knife was in that pool now, probably rusted and useless, a symbol of his own lack of courage.

To pass the initiation Tom had to retrieve the knife from the pool, and to do that he would have to enter the Black Tunnel. He'd have to stumble and grope his way through half a kilometre of cold, dripping darkness to the smaller tunnel, penetrating the very heart of the Escarpment. Turning his back on the cliff, he strode angrily towards the waterfall. Well, he was going now to get that useless, rusted jack-knife. He would finish the initiation and overcome all his nightmare terrors.

He heard the roar of the waterfall as he clambered up the steep, gravelly hill. He didn't look up because he knew the cold, black, mocking mouth of the Tunnel would be there, silent and unmoving.

It would always be there, waiting for him. Like a great, evil, crouching beast it would be waiting for him to walk into its yawning, sweating mouth. And he *would* walk into its mouth — into the darkness that in his fears went on for a crushing eternity.

He stood before the indifferent, gaping blackness. There was no change in it since the last time. There never would be a change. The icy draft of air issuing from the depths of the Escarpment; the scarred, sweating rocks; the old grille submerged in the cold water, bit by bit rusting away — it was all the same.

Steadily Tom faced the Tunnel, daring himself to walk into its blackness and retrieve the rusty dime-store jack-knife.

2
A friend at last

As he faced the Black Tunnel, Tom's surroundings faded into nothingness. He felt only the push of cold air coming from the opening; he heard nothing but the almost inaudible *drip, drip* as beads of moisture fell into the pool that covered the floor of the passage.

Tom took a deep breath, swallowed and forced his feet to shuffle forward. He placed one foot slowly in front of the other. Cold water and slime squelched into his sneakers and dampened the cuffs of his jeans.

One foot, then the other foot. The dank air brushing his cheek. The slow, even *drip, drip, drip* of the sweating blackness. The blackness. The deep, crushing, wet blackness.

And then Tom could go no farther. He tried to fight the horror of that closed-in blackness, but it welled from his stomach, reached up through his lungs and locked his mouth. He choked, and dizzy flashes shot through his eyes. Beads of sweat fell from his face and joined the slow drip from the sweating Tunnel.

Be brave, he screamed in his mind. There's nothing to be scared of. Nothing . . .

Then the blind panic, the uncontrollable, surging panic grabbed him. He screamed, but only a small sound came out. He whipped around and ran.

"Hey! Watch it!" someone cried. Tom smashed into a body and they both slipped and crashed into the mud.

The collision jarred Tom's mind back into focus. A half-familiar face peered at him. A gangly boy, maybe a year or two older than himself, lay on the ground beside him.

"You were watching me!" Tom shouted wildly. He jumped up, ready to smash the intruder's face. But the mud clung to his sneakers and he slipped again.

"I wasn't," the boy said. "I spoke to you but you didn't seem to hear me. Then you turned around and crashed right into me."

A feeling of humiliation and hatred surged through Tom's body. Someone had seen him run like a little baby from nothing. He glanced sideways at the boy, who was trying to steady his legs and get back on his feet again. His face held a look of intense concentration.

Finally he looked at Tom and then back at the ground, grinning shyly. Tom started to relax, his mind eased by the other's awkward shyness. The boy seemed to have no intention of laughing.

Tom stood up and held out a muddy hand. The other boy grasped it and hauled himself to his feet.

"Do you always fall down like that?" Tom asked with a testing smile.

The boy peered at him for a second, blushed a bit, and then smiled and spoke with surprising firmness. "Always," he said. "I mean, I'm forever falling all over things, and I can barely tie my own shoelaces. It's my terrible co-ordination.

"I've always been like this," he added. "When I was little the doctors said I'd outgrow it." He shrugged his shoulders. "I don't know, though. Nothing's improved yet as far as I can tell. But I guess everyone has something to struggle with. For me it's co-ordination."

Tom gazed at the boy in bewilderment, not sure what he was talking about. The guy seemed a little weird, but at least he wasn't snickering "chicken."

The other boy noticed Tom's doubtful look and blushed thoroughly.

"What I mean," he said anxiously, trying to make himself clear, "is that my mind tells my hands, for instance, to do something, but the message gets a little mixed up on the way down and so my hands either miss what they're supposed to be doing, or do it a little jerkily. It's just that my body won't always do what my mind tells it to."

"I have the same problem," Tom muttered bitterly, thinking about his wild flight every time he was faced with a dark, closed-in space.

"You mean you're unco-ordinated too?" the boy demanded hopefully.

Tom shook his head. Suddenly he couldn't hold it in any longer. With a jerky movement of his arms he blurted out, "No. I ran from the Tunnel — just like a stupid little kid — because I couldn't stand the blackness. My mind told my feet to go forward but instead I ran away."

Tom gritted his teeth and waited for a howl of derision. The boy looked at him amiably and nodded.

"Oh, that's emotional, not physical," he said matter-of-factly, as though all points were now cleared up. "It sounds as though you've got claustrophobia."

Tom looked at him in amazement, but the other boy had picked up a knapsack lying on a rock at the side of the Tunnel. He was trying to fit it onto his back. Automatically Tom helped him slide it onto his bony shoulders.

"Thanks," he said. Then in a voice attempting to sound casual he added, "I guess you don't remember me. I'm Andrew MacDonald. You know, my dad runs the pharmacy. I guess you haven't seen me for about three years, so of course you don't remember me. You played ball with me once."

Andrew looked at Tom hopefully, and suddenly Tom remembered why his face looked so familiar. Andrew was considered one of the town's "personalities," even though nobody really knew him. He was usually at school in Toronto because, according to his extremely proud father, all his IQ tests indicated he was a genius. He didn't look like a genius; but then Tom had never seen a genius, except as a crazy professor type in science fiction movies.

Tom remembered the afternoon a few years ago when he had tried to teach Andrew to throw a ball properly. Now he knew why it had been so impossible.

"Yeah, I remember," he said. "Are you still that rotten at playing ball?"

Andrew grinned and relaxed. "Nope," he said eagerly. "I've practised a lot so most of the time I can pitch fairly accurately."

"Maybe we can throw a ball around some afternoon then," Tom suggested as casually as possible. It would be great to have someone — even Andrew — to do things with now and then.

Andrew agreed quickly, and with flattering eagerness proposed the next afternoon.

A year ago, Tom thought, he would have been polite to Andrew if he'd met him again, but he would never have even considered asking him to play ball. But a year of loneliness had changed everything. Andrew was someone near his own age and that was important. Besides, the other boy was lonely too. After all, he wasn't the type Billy would invite to join the Cobras. They would be a couple of outcasts together.

Tom sighed as he thought of always being the odd man out. He still couldn't believe all that had happened to him. Before Billy had moved into the area, he had been the leader. Since he was good at both sports and school work, all the boys had looked up to him. Then Billy came and talked them into having a real gang. He was jealous of Tom, but since Tom could do things better and fight better, Billy was forced to give him the lead.

Tom had agreed when Billy had said they should have an initiation into the gang. But then Billy had made the initiation a trip through the tunnels in the gorge. Everyone had to go through the tunnels; they had to go alone; and they had to go in complete darkness.

Tom had scoffed at the initiation, had said it was for babies. But then everyone — even cowardly little Skinner — had done it. Everyone, that is, but Tom.

Billy had looked him in the eye, and a slow smile had spread across his face. "You're chicken!" he had said in a soft, silky voice. "You're no Cobra, Kirby. You're just a chicken!"

They had all taken up the cry of "Chicken!" and in one afternoon, as the word spread, Tom had become a social outcast. No one would be caught dead with "Chicken Man."

Tom shoved the bitter memory into the back of his mind as he and Andrew scrambled back down to the river bank. Sometimes as they moved through the gorge

Tom had to give the other boy a hand to get him back on his feet when he tripped over a tree root or a rock. Before long they'd made it into a joke and were both laughing over his frequent sprawls.

With a stroke of what Tom considered to be pure personal genius, he offered to take a turn with the heavy knapsack. As he adjusted the straps to fit his shoulders, he demanded jokingly "What do you have in this thing — rocks?"

Andrew grinned. "Well," he said, "as a matter of fact, they are rocks. Fossils."

Tom looked at him in wry disgust.

"I'm an amateur geologist," Andrew explained. "That's what I was doing down here, collecting rock samples. There aren't many varieties, mostly just limestone. But there are a lot of interesting possibilities for fossils. Many of the best fossils are found embedded in limestone, you know," he said eagerly.

Tom admitted he didn't know, seeing as fossils had never occupied much of his thinking time. "And," he added, "if you think you're going to rook me into being your faithful bearer while you pick up half the rocks on the Escarpment, you're nuts."

They laughed again, and that seemed to Tom the beginning of their friendship. Andrew was different from the other boys, maybe, and half the time you didn't know what he was talking about, but still there was something about him that Tom liked. The past year had made him a lot less choosy.

At the edge of a small waterfall they sat down, and without saying anything, watched the tumbling river. Tom threw some dead wood in, fascinated by the way the water tossed it around, submerged it, then finally discarded it on the bank farther down the stream. He always found rushing water intriguing. Andrew suddenly began digging in his knapsack and fished out a large brown paper bag.

"Lunch," he said. "My mother's been trying to fatten me up ever since I got back from school last week, so there's lots."

After the boys had devoured the rock-mashed sandwiches and cake, they lazed in the hot sun for almost an hour, watching the more daring of the birds peck at the crumbs they tossed. Then they stripped off their clothes and swam in the swirling pool at the foot of the big waterfall, finally perching on a ledge of slippery rock behind the falls, delighted with themselves because no one could see them.

Andrew was perfectly at home in the water. "Look at this," he called to Tom. Quickly he turned an underwater somersault.

"I should be a fish or a frog," he yelled gleefully when his head bobbed up again. "I can do anything in the water!"

Tom splashed him and Andrew dived, pulling Tom under by one foot. They came up spluttering and shouting like a couple of savages.

At last they tired of swimming. After drying out in the warmth of a sun-heated rock, they took the easier, roundabout way back up the cliff. Their muscles ached with the exertion of the day.

At the top, Andrew pulled his bicycle from some bushes not far from where Tom had hidden his. It was a new ten-speed, Tom noted with envy. Andrew wheeled it over proudly.

"I got it for Christmas last year," he said, "and this week is the first I've used it. Man, can it go fast. That is," he added with a grin, "if I don't let my feet slip off the pedals. I'm going to have to get those straps racers use to keep their feet in."

"Well, if you have too much trouble using it and decide to throw it away, throw it in my direction," Tom joked. It really was a beautiful bike, and Tom was just itching to try it out.

They pedalled down the laneway to the road. Mr. Piers was still outside when they passed the mill, and Tom was amazed to see Andrew wave to him. He hadn't known anyone under forty was on good terms with Mr. Piers. "He plays chess with my father on Sunday afternoons," Andrew explained when he saw Tom's startled look.

They rode along the top of the Escarpment in silence.

The earlier heat waves were gone, replaced by the slight chill of an evening breeze. The sun was beginning to set.

"We must be late," Tom commented without concern. His parents would be too pleased that he'd made a friend to worry about his being late for dinner.

At the top of the hill where the road suddenly led down the Escarpment, Andrew scrambled off his bicycle.

"What's up?" Tom asked.

"The hill's too steep for me. I'm not used to the ten-speed yet," Andrew explained. "I've already gone flying on a smaller hill this week. Say," he added, "if you want to ride my bike down, I'll walk yours for you."

Tom felt rotten about leaving Andrew to walk down the hill, but he couldn't resist the idea of trying out the bike. "You sure you don't mind?" he asked anxiously as he threw his leg over the seat. The bike seemed to weigh about half what his own did.

"Nope," the other boy said. "There's no reason why you should walk just because I do. Meet me in front of the pharmacy."

Tom nodded, then pushed off. The cool wind bit through his clothes and he could feel goosebumps all over his body. He couldn't hear anything but the cool *whoosh* of air. The pressure of the speed pushed against his eyelids like a cool, gentle hand, pressing them closed. The bicycle responded quickly, easily. He tried changing gears. His lungs were pressed full of the clean air and he felt he could ride like this forever.

Finally he reached town, and without pedalling once, pulled up at the pharmacy. It was still open. Tom looked back up the road, but Andrew wasn't in sight. He felt guilty about leaving his friend to plod down the hill when he could have flown down on his bicycle. But with a grin Tom admitted to himself he would have let Andrew walk down fifty times before he would have given up that ride.

Tom sat on the steps for awhile and admired the lines of the bicycle, wishing he had one like it. But since his old bike was in perfect running order, he knew his parents wouldn't buy him a new one. Regretfully Tom dwelt on the problem of not being a couple of years older. If he were even fourteen he might be able to talk his parents into letting him pick fruit for the farmers. They always said he was still too young for such hard work, and he should just enjoy his holidays while he could. But boy, he could enjoy them a lot more with this kind of bicycle.

He looked down the road again. Andrew was just coming into sight, patiently trudging along pushing Tom's bike. Tom felt another surge of mild guilt. He fished into his pocket for some change and went to the pop machine just inside the door of the pharmacy. He picked out an orange and a coke. He liked both, so he'd let Andrew choose.

Andrew was putting the bike on its kickstand when Tom came out with the pop. He chose the orange, tilted his head back and let it fizzle down his throat. "Boy, does that taste good," he said, wiping his mouth on his sleeve.

They sat on the steps and finished their drinks in comfortable silence. Finally Tom got up. "Well, see you tomorrow," he said. The words felt good because it had been such a long time since he'd said them.

3
What's a million
years or so?

When Tom woke up the next morning he felt good. The sun was shining through his window and Andrew was going to meet him after lunch at the ball diamond. The world was better than it had been for quite awhile.

"Tom! Breakfast!" his mother called cheerfully from the foot of the stairs. "No lazing around in bed this morning, young man! There are chores for you to do."

Tom groaned. What a dummy he was. For a couple of weeks now he'd been putting off all the little jobs he was supposed to do. Yesterday morning — a thousand years ago, before he'd met Andrew — he'd finally promised his mother he would do all of them today.

Well, nothing like a bit of enthusiasm to soften the old folks up, he thought with a grin. He dragged himself out of bed and got washed and dressed with so much speed that his mother had to call him only twice more for breakfast.

Tom bounded down the stairs, but he slipped and fell

on a scatter rug at the bottom and went flying. He stood up with a groan. This was not a good start.

Since his father had not yet left for work, Tom figured he could really impress both his parents with one display of enthusiasm. "Well," he said brightly, "what's on the list for today? I guess things must have been stacking up."

They looked at him. His father stood up and put a hand against his son's forehead. "He's not feverish," he said in mock amazement.

"Aw, come on," Tom protested. "I'm just getting myself ready to do all those chores and you make a big deal about it."

He tried to look injured but finally laughed with his parents.

"Well, I wouldn't want all that eagerness to go to waste," his mother said, "so you can start with washing the porch windows. Then there's the grass to cut, the hedges to trim, the garden to weed and water . . . Shall I stop, or can you take it all before breakfast?"

"There's that much to do?" Tom said in dismay. He should have known it would pile up like that. Just when he had something good to do, too.

"Well, if you've nothing else on, today's a good day to get started," his father said.

Tom knew they'd been pretty worried about the way he never did anything with anyone any more. They'd even made him go to the doctor for a checkup to see if he was sick. How could he tell them no one would have anything to do with him because he was a chicken?

"The only thing is," Tom said unhappily, "I sort of forgot all about this and promised a guy I'd meet him this afternoon to play ball for awhile."

His parents exchanged glances.

"Well," his mother said, looking at Tom's father, "we don't want you to think you can put things off forever, but if you wash the windows this morning, and maybe water the garden, the other things can wait one more day."

His father nodded.

"Gee, thanks," Tom exclaimed in relief. He was grateful they would let him go, just as he had been grateful they didn't bug him when he never went anywhere.

"Just until tomorrow, remember," his father said as he stood up from the table. "See you tonight."

He kissed his wife, picked up his briefcase and went whistling out the side door. The door squeaked as it swung shut and Tom resolved to find the oil can and oil the hinge before anyone asked him to.

After breakfast he went to work on the windows. It took a long time because they were coated with dirt, but he didn't mind. Work didn't seem so bad when he had something to look forward to later on.

When he was finished, he took out his bicycle and set off towards town. Since the baseball diamond was just on the outskirts, it took only about fifteen minutes to get there. Tom wondered if he could have made it in less than ten with a racer.

Andrew was waiting for him when he arrived. He looked relieved when he saw Tom ride up.

"Am I late?" Tom asked. "I had a bunch of chores to do before I could come."

"Oh, no," Andrew said. "I think I was probably early. I was afraid you might have forgotten."

Tom was pleased. Although he didn't want to show it, he'd been afraid Andrew would forget their plans too. "Well, let's pitch for awhile," he said casually.

Andrew nodded, then loped off a short distance.

"Go farther back!" Tom yelled. There wasn't any challenge that close up.

Andrew hesitated, but finally moved back. Tom gauged the distance and threw the ball.

It went right to Andrew, but as he leaped for it, he stumbled, did a wild half-twist and fell to the ground. Somehow in the process he had caught the ball, but when he fell it dropped out of his mitt.

Tom sighed. Andrew was better than he'd been four years ago, but it was obvious that his co-ordination was pretty bad. With a flush of embarrassment, Tom hoped fervently that none of the other boys would go by while they were playing.

"You okay?" he yelled. Andrew nodded and stood up, brushing his jeans.

Then he wound up to throw the ball back. First he stood absolutely straight. His hands dangled loosely at his sides while he judged the distance, but he held his neck at an angle so that his chin jutted forward. Then as he pulled back his arm to pitch, his body seemed to coil up and bend backwards in the middle. Finally, with a sudden jerky motion, his arm swung up and over his head like a windmill and he released the ball.

Miraculously, Tom thought, it came directly to him. It didn't whack its way into the mitt, but it got there.

"Nice pitch!" he shouted.

They threw the ball back and forth for nearly an hour. Just when they had decided to go, Tom suddenly caught sight of Billy MacPherson watching them, his arms folded across the handlebars of his bike.

Tom's eyes narrowed and he stared challengingly at Billy.

"Seen your knife lately?" Billy called, his voice twisted into tones of friendly interest. Tom tried to think of something cutting to say, but couldn't.

"No, not lately," was all he could come up with. He tried to compensate by staring Billy down. But the other boy just laughed, and after looking hard at Andrew for a moment, got on his bike and rode away.

Andrew came up behind Tom. "Who's that?" he asked. "I don't think I've seen him before."

Tom wanted to tell Andrew to keep away from Billy, and to list in venomous detail all his personality flaws, but he knew from past experience that he would just sound jealous. And Andrew still didn't know about the initiation, since Tom was reluctant to talk about his own failure. So he replied as casually as he could, "Oh, he's just a new guy. Lives in the house at the end of our road. You know, the big flashy one that was built a couple of years ago."

For a moment he was afraid Andrew would ask more, but he just shrugged and invited Tom to come home for a bottle of pop. Tom accepted with a guilty twinge of relief, and forced all thoughts of Billy out of his mind.

Andrew's house was much the same as Tom's — very old, very beautiful and painted white, with a pinkish-red roof. Andrew's mother even complained the way Tom's mother did about the incredible inconvenience of it.

"I don't understand how anyone with any understanding of how a house is run could have designed it this way. Of course, it was different then when everyone had hired help."

Mrs. MacDonald rattled on. "Do you boys want another piece of cake? I thought boys your age were bottomless pits. Well, Andrew certainly isn't, are you, dear?" She whisked out of the kitchen for a minute, but the flow of her chatter didn't stop.

"Would you like — " Andrew began, but his mother had hurried back into the room, talking all the while.

"Andrew, dear, I wish you would clean the crumbs off your plate. Are you sure you won't have another piece, Tom? Your mother's lucky you aren't a picky eater the way Andrew is. It's no wonder he's all skin and bones — I worry about him. But I'm pleased he's found such a nice friend."

She stopped and beamed at Tom. Totally embarrassed, he had no idea what to say. He stole a glance at Andrew, expecting him to be even more embarrassed than he was. But instead, his friend wore a look of unholy amusement. Tom glared.

"Well, my mother says I'm picky too," he finally spluttered.

"Oh, I'm sure that's not so," Mrs. MacDonald said. "I'm sure no one could be as fussy as Andrew. He's a good boy, but fussy. Aren't you, dear?"

Andrew grinned at his mother. "Terribly fussy, Mom. In fact, I think you should disown me."

"Oh, don't be so silly, dear."

"Tom and I are going to go look at my rocks now," Andrew announced.

Tom marvelled at the way he spoke so firmly to his mother. He had thought someone as shy as Andrew would be crawling with humiliation from his mother's continual fussing.

"She's just excited because I'm home," Andrew explained, as they went upstairs, "and I don't get home much. Besides, I'm not usually very good at making friends."

"Yeah, my mother worries about me not having friends too," Tom said. "Parents always worry about something."

With the old ground re-established, Tom wondered why they were going to see Andrew's rocks. He had said he was an amateur geologist, but who cared about that? Why look at a bunch of rocks? You could see rocks anywhere.

"My collection is in my den here," Andrew said as he led the way. "I have too many for my bedroom now, so my parents let me turn one of the spare bedrooms into a den."

Tom was a lot more interested in the idea of a den all his own than in rocks, but when he walked into the room and Andrew switched on the light, he was surprised.

Shelves of glass lined all but one of the wood-panelled walls. An old desk with a pile of books, a microscope and some chemicals took up the empty wall. Here and there on the shelves pieces of blue and black velvet cloth held bits of glimmering crystal formations or abstract-patterned rocks. On a table in the centre of the room was a huge piece of shimmering quartz about seventy-five centimetres wide and fifty high.

But it wasn't the kind of quartz Tom knew — the little white or pink rocks found lying about in gravel. These were huge geometric crystals shooting out like sculptured icicles, like cold crystal plants yearning towards the light.

The largest crystal was about twenty-five centimetres long and eight across, while the others ranged down to tiny ones, still identical in shape. They clustered and thrust outward from a base of crystal rock.

Tom ran his hands over the six-sided crystals, smooth and cool and almost razor sharp at the edges. Then he quickly pulled back.

"Gee, sorry," he said as Andrew grinned at him. "I mean, is it fragile? Can you touch it?"

"Well, if it were dropped or yanked, the crystals might break off." Andrew ran his own fingers over the sharp, clean points of the quartz crystals. "But it is rock, after all, so it's pretty sturdy."

"Where'd you find it?" Tom demanded. He had visions of going off and finding something like it for his own bedroom.

"I didn't find it myself," Andrew explained. "I half traded and half bought it with a prize I won at school. I had two excellent samples of one type of mineral that I found last summer on a rock hunting trip with one of my teachers. So I traded one of them, plus the prize, for this specimen I found in a rock collector's shop near Bancroft. It's fairly rare to find a cluster of such large, perfectly formed crystals."

"What did you trade for it?"

"This is it here, or rather a specimen like it." Andrew pointed out a rock slightly smaller than a fist. It was spotted, with tufts of something sprouting outwards, making it look like a miniature yellow porcupine or a spiny moss of some sort.

"It's called Uranophane," Andrew explained, picking the rock up very carefully, almost lovingly. "This is a very large specimen for this type of mineral. It forms as an alteration of other uranium-type minerals over a fracture in the rock. In most specimens the needles are less than two centimetres long, but the longest of these are almost three. It's a very soft mineral, so you have to be careful with it."

He handed it to Tom who held it gingerly, feeling the hard but delicate prickle of the mineral against his palms. Then he carefully laid it back on the black velvet.

"Wow," he said, "I didn't know rocks came this way."

Andrew grinned. "Most of the ones around here don't," he said. "And you don't just stumble over good specimens, you know. You have to look for them, and even then you can't find every kind of rock just anywhere. Once you find a good specimen, it still has to be cleaned." He pointed to a variety of rocks on one shelf. "These all came from up around Bancroft, not too far from the Haliburton area. They're all different types of mineral formations caused by volcanoes — or by magma breaking through the earth's crust, or cooling below the crust and slowly working towards the surface. It's considered a very unusual area, geologically."

He smiled, obviously pleased with his collection.

Tom felt lost. He was pretty good in science at school, but he couldn't remember ever talking about rocks becoming so beautiful because of volcanoes.

"There haven't been any volcanoes around here for a long time, have there?" he asked suspiciously. He hadn't understood everything his friend had said and for a moment he was afraid he might be having his leg pulled.

"Well," Andrew said, "the quartz on the table is considered one of the youngest rock specimens from the area. You can tell, because it would have had to cool very slowly to make crystals that large. It's supposed to be only about a billion years old."

"A *billion?*" Tom gasped. He felt as though his concept of the world was rocking at the foundations. His mind couldn't grasp the idea of something that had been created a billion years ago sitting on the table in front of him. That chunk of rock and crystal had been made over a billion years ago!

"How old are the others?"

"Hard to say," Andrew said seriously. "When things are that old, they have to guess. Some of them are dated at about thirteen hundred million years. They're the oldest from the Bancroft area. But all the rocks are considered younger than the rocks farther north, up in the Canadian Shield."

"Well, what's a million years or so here or there," Tom joked.

He walked slowly around the shelves, practically forgetting all about Andrew. He picked up and felt first one rock and then another. They were every colour — from shiny, deep black and a deep royal blue, right through to scarlets and a deep translucent green. They were all so solid, so heavy, as though every one of the millions of years could be felt through their hard, rough or smooth surfaces.

He came to one he found particularly beautiful. It looked as though it had been a round ball, split cleanly in half, then covered with a coat of varnish. Inside were ring upon ring of soft purples, sand browns and rich reds all melting into each other. It was as large as a softball.

"That's a geode from Mexico," Andrew said. "They're very common there. In fact, the guy who sold it to me said they're lying around all over the desert."

Tom didn't say anything. The thought of a billion years was still revolving in his mind, making him feel as though anything he had to say was very trivial.

Andrew smiled shyly. "If you like it, you can have it. I have lots more. In fact I'm going to sell them to tourists at the flea market on weekends. They make super bookends when they're cut and polished like that."

"You're sure?" Tom demanded.

"Yeah, I'm sure. I'd like you to have it. I really would."

Tom felt the same way he had when he'd borrowed Andrew's bicycle. He couldn't give it up. Riding home that evening, he felt great. He wondered if his parents would be impressed with the geode. And he wondered why he had thought Andrew was such a goof. So what if he couldn't play baseball? He knew all about things that had happened over a billion years ago. Billy MacPherson sure didn't know anything like that.

4
The Cobras

The roar of the lawn mower sounded good to Tom that evening as it blended with his whistling. His parents hadn't even asked him to cut the lawn before it got dark, but if Andrew had something planned for the next day it would be rotten to have to stay home and do chores. At least this way, Tom figured, he had a head start. Maybe they could even head towards the Escarpment and look for some fossils. He was sure he knew a hundred hidden gorges and crevices that Andrew would never have found on his own.

Tom didn't hear the bicycle on the gravel driveway. He turned the mower to do one more sweep along the edge of the lawn, and suddenly he was face to face with Billy MacPherson. He stopped dead; then very casually he leaned down and switched off the motor. Arms crossed, he leaned his elbows on the handle of the mower.

"How you doing, Chicken Man?" Billy sneered.

"This is private property and nobody invited you,"

Tom said. Billy wasn't going to get the best of him this time.

"So don't get unfriendly." Billy wore a mock-injured look. "I came to do you a favour — just to show that, though I can't stand chickens, at least I give 'em a chance."

"Take off, MacPherson, before I have to send you crying home to your mother with another black eye and bloody nose," Tom ordered.

Billy's eyes narrowed at the jibe over their earlier fight. They both knew he wouldn't go through that again if he could help it. They glared at each other.

"Hold on, Chicken Man," Billy said at last. "I just dropped over to save you some trouble. If you were maybe planning to ride all the way to town to see that goofy friend of yours tomorrow, you may as well forget it. He's coming with the Cobras. My dad's taking us all fishing and for a barbecue, and Andrew's coming too. All the regular guys are coming. You aren't invited, of course."

Tom lunged, but Billy jumped easily aside. He laughed.

"You're losing your touch, Chicken Man," he mocked. "And by the way, you may as well forget about ever doing anything with Andrew again, because just in case he doesn't know the facts, we're going to tell him everything about you, Chicken Man. He's smart, so he'll know you aren't worth talking to. I like guys with brains, so I figure I might even offer to make him vice-president of the Cobras."

Laughing, Billy ran back to his bicycle. Tom started after him. Just one good punch in Billy's fat face. Just one!

"You don't know what you're talking about, Mac-Pherson!" he yelled.

But Billy just shouted over his shoulder, "See ya, Chicken Man!"

Tom stood for a minute in the darkening shadows. Viciously he picked up a handful of gravel and threw it down the road after Billy, who was by then well out of range. Tom didn't know whether he was going to cry or throw up. Billy! He wished he had run the lawn mower over him — or better yet that he could throw him over the big waterfall and watch him bounce and scream over the rocks at the bottom. Billy had wrecked everything before, and now he was even going to wreck his friendship with Andrew.

"So who cares!" Tom shouted at everyone and no one. The dark trees bowed with a sudden gust of wind, as though agreeing with him.

"So who cares!" he yelled again. He picked up a fallen branch and swung it at the trunk of the big willow, punctuating every word until the branch broke into little bits.

"Who . . . gives . . . one . . . damn . . . care!"

Tom spat out. If his parents heard him swear, he knew he'd get it. But that just gave him a perverse satisfaction.

The sun had sunk, leaving dark, deep-green shadows. Tom ran into the orchard by the old carriage house and tried to kick up tufts of sod. Furiously he tore clumps of unripe cherries from the trees and threw them wildly into the air.

Finally he was exhausted. It was no use. It had to happen. Andrew would have found out about him sooner or later, and that would have ended everything anyhow. For the rest of his life people would find out what was wrong with him — how frightened he was, how even a room with the lights turned off at night gave him a feeling of cold, clammy hands groping for control of his mind.

Why was he so frightened? No, not frightened — terrified. He was blindly, madly terrified of dark, closed-in spaces. Other people weren't. Why him? For maybe the thousandth time Tom turned it inside out in his mind. He didn't have any idea this time either. Maybe he was just crazy.

He wandered back to finish mowing the lawn. He could barely see what he was doing, but he didn't really care. Finally his mother called from the house, "Time to come in, Tom. There's fresh banana bread."

But even his favourite snack didn't change how he

felt. He tried to act cheerful, but his parents weren't fooled.

"Anything wrong, Tom? Are you feeling all right?" his mother asked.

"If there's anything bothering you, we'd appreciate your telling us. That's what we're here for, after all," Tom's father added, trying to sound casual.

Tom looked down at the floor, wishing he could tell them what was wrong. But how could he tell them what a loser he was? He wished for a minute he had a brother or sister who could blab it for him when he wasn't there to see all the disgust and embarrassment they would be sure to feel when they found out about him. There was no way he could tell them himself.

"Oh, I just have a headache," he lied.

"You're sure that's all?" his father asked.

Tom looked at him miserably, then nodded. "Yeah, that's all. Guess I'll go to bed."

His mother made a move as though to stop him, but he brushed by her and ran upstairs. He hurried into his pyjamas, then got into bed before leaning over to turn out the light. Tom shut his eyes for a minute so they'd get used to the dark and it wouldn't seem so black in his room. When he opened them again, they were adjusted; the shadows caused by the moonlight streaming in his window were familiar and almost friendly.

The shadows were always the same in his room because he always kept everything where it belonged rather than lie in bed and stare at some grotesquely exaggerated shadow until his mind could identify what caused it. There was a new shape that night, a large, round one made by the geode Andrew had given him. Tom squeezed his eyes shut, but he couldn't stop himself. Warm tears slipped out and ran down his cheeks.

It had been a long, long time since he had cried about anything. He was almost thirteen, after all. Stop it! he told himself fiercely. But it didn't do any good. The tears kept rolling down his cheeks and dripping onto his pillow.

It was late before he finally fell asleep. And he must have cried a lot — an awful lot, he figured — because his pillow was still a little damp when he woke up the next morning.

That day was a bad day. In fact, Tom thought bitterly, it was a horrendous day, a terrible day, a rotten day, an incredibly ghastly day. And worst of all, it was a Saturday.

Tom hoped that it would rain — or better still, snow, sleet and hail. But after listening to the weather report on the radio and staring at the blue, almost cloudless sky, he realized that the day was perfect for a fishing trip and barbecue.

Moodily he began to weed the garden. There was some satisfaction in ripping the weeds out by the roots, but not much. The chores seemed to stretch endlessly ahead of him.

Surprisingly, though, the day didn't get worse. How could things get worse, Tom thought, when they'd already reached rock bottom?

His father challenged him to a game of darts, and then they practised pitching for almost an hour. By evening Tom was beginning to feel almost cheerful. Maybe Andrew wouldn't like Billy. After all, who *could* like Billy?

Tom decided to look for garter snakes along the road. As he strolled across the lawn, he thought almost cheerfully of all the things Andrew would probably find to hate Billy for. But then he heard the sound of a car and looked up just in time to see the MacPherson station wagon go by. Andrew was in the front seat between Billy and his father. The rest of the gang were in the back.

Tom stared after them. Despite everything, somehow he hadn't really believed that Andrew would go with the Cobras. Billy and the others wouldn't care that Andrew had a rock a billion years old. But how could he know they were being friendly just to spite Tom? Anyhow, he wouldn't want to hang around with Tom now that he'd heard what a chicken he was.

Tom wandered around the orchards for awhile, then decided he might as well go to bed. What did he have to stay up for anyhow?

Too miserable to care, he dropped his clothes onto a

chair as he undressed. When he flicked off the light and looked around the room, all the familiar shadows were there. The moonlight shone clear, ice-white across the polished floor — then unexpectedly dissolved into large, twisted lumps of shadows that seemed to move just the tiniest fraction of an inch as Tom watched them. He felt the same gnawing panic he had felt in the face of the Black Tunnel. He squeezed his eyes shut and fought the waves of terror. Stupid! It was just the shadows from his clothes. There wasn't anything to be scared of.

He opened his eyes. A flying lump of blackness came hurtling through the air at him. He made a sound half gasp, half groan — and hit out with his hands as the thing thumped onto his stomach.

Meow!

"Mitzit, you dumb cat!" Tom sighed with relief. His fingers stroked the cat's back and burrowed into the fluffed fur. He must have left his door open a crack.

"You dumb cat," he said again as he snuggled under the blankets. Mitzit circled daintily for a minute, then thumped herself down beside him.

The cat's rasping purr floated in and out of Tom's mind as he drifted off to sleep. Bit by bit the sound became louder, harsher, grating on his ears. Looking around, he could vaguely make out rows of bleachers filled with a noisy, seething crowd. Tom seemed to be standing at home plate, holding a huge bat. He looked up and saw Andrew wearing a T-shirt with a huge, luminous, purple cobra emblazoned across it.

Silently Andrew stared at him; then a cruel, twisted sneer came over his face. "Hey there, Chicken Man. Now you're going to play ball our way."

The people in the stands, all wearing purple cobra T-shirts, began laughing and jeering. His parents and an aunt he hadn't seen in years were laughing more loudly than anyone else.

Tom glanced behind him and came face to face with another cobra — a green one on a black T-shirt. Shrinking back a step, he looked up. From behind a huge catcher's mask Billy's eyes gleamed wickedly. Billy snickered and Tom turned quickly away.

Andrew was winding up, just like a professional pitcher. Slowly he let go of the ball and it drifted towards Tom. Tom pulled the bat off his shoulder and dragged it into a swing — but the ball kept coming. He swung again. Still the ball came floating towards him, and again and again he tried to hit it. Finally there was a thud, and the ball sailed heavily through the air and disappeared into a hole in a green wooden fence that somehow hadn't been there before.

Tom stood and watched it disappear, then looked for bases to run to. There weren't any. Andrew turned towards him. "You hit that all wrong," he said in contempt.

"You have to get it or else you're out," Billy said

gleefully, the green cobra swelling on his chest.

Slowly Tom ran towards the fence and the little black hole where the ball had rolled in. As he got closer, the hole grew; it became a huge tunnel mouth.

Tom could see the ball lying inside the shadow of the tunnel. Laughing out loud, he ran in after it. He bent down and reached for it, but it was gone. Frightened now, Tom turned to leave the tunnel — but the entrance too was gone.

Everywhere was blackness. He began to scream and thrash his arms. Everything was muffled, closing in, squeezing him. He was in the cupped palms of some faceless giant who was slowly closing his hands — squeezing him like a squashed bug in the blackness.

Tom screamed and screamed. Then someone was shaking him. His eyes flew open. The lights were on in his room and his parents were bending over him.

"Tom!" his mother was shouting. "Wake up! Tom, wake up! You're having a nightmare!"

Tom looked around. Mitzit was crouched in one corner of the room, eyes wide, staring at him. His father and mother were seated, one on each side of his bed, in their pyjamas.

"Are you all right, Tom?" his father asked gently, stroking his hair.

His mother hugged him, and all of a sudden Tom started to cry. Somehow he forced out a description of the terrible, squeezing blackness. His mother hugged him again and neither of them said anything more until his crying had subsided and he started hiccupping. His father gave him a glass of water and a handkerchief.

"I'm sorry," Tom muttered. But it didn't really matter that his parents had seen him crying like a tiny baby.

"Oh, Tom," his mother said gently, "what are you sorry for? We had hoped that you were over your claustrophobia, but there's nothing to be sorry for."

"Everybody has a dream now and then that leaves him feeling as if his insides have been torn out," his father said. "It's been a long time, though, since you've had that dream about the giant squeezing you."

Tom was exhausted. For a moment he said nothing and felt nothing. Finally, half crying, he muttered, "But why am I so stupid about things being dark and closed in?"

"You don't remember," his father asked, "about the time you were locked in the root cellar?"

Tom looked up in surprise and shook his head.

"You were just about two years old," his mother explained slowly, "when we had some friends drop in one afternoon. They had a boy about five who was a little hellion. We all thought you two were out in the back yard playing but when they were ready to leave they discovered Eddy was missing.

"It took us a long time to find him and when we did you weren't with him. It turned out that he'd got tired of playing with you and had shut you in the storage cupboard in the root cellar. We didn't hear you screaming. By the time we found you, you were completely hysterical. The doctor had to give you a sedative and it was months before you would stay in a darkened room without becoming hysterical again.

"You remember you were eight before you started sleeping without a night light. We thought you were over your claustrophobia because after you told us to take the night light out of your room you never mentioned it again. And you haven't had that giant dream for about three years."

Tom looked at his parents but he found it hard to think. He couldn't remember being locked in the cupboard, but the dread of it — even thinking of it — numbed him. "How long was I in there?" he asked finally.

"About an hour and a half as near as we could figure," his father said gently. "It was a terrible thing to happen to a baby. You were still too small to reach the latch, so you couldn't let yourself out. The doctor said then that it would take you a long time to get over it, and he was right. We hoped when you said you didn't want the light any more that you'd licked it."

Tom shook his head. "No. The kids at school were

talking about some other kid who still had a night light and what a baby he was. So I told you to take mine away in case they found out and thought I was a baby too. I thought you'd be ashamed of me if I said I didn't — well — like the dark."

"We'd never be ashamed of you for that, stupid." His mother laughed and kissed the top of his head. "Especially since you've tried so hard to get over it on your own. Are you all right now?"

Tom nodded and snuggled back into the bed. Mitzit took a flying leap and landed on his stomach again.

"Tell us when things are bothering you, Tom," his father said as he left the room. "Do you want the light left on?"

Tom desperately wanted it left on, but he couldn't say so. He hesitated for a moment, then shook his head. "No," he said. "I'm not a baby."

He could see his father smile before flicking the light switch. Tom burrowed his fingers into Mitzit's fur and sighed. There were so many dark places everywhere.

5
Fruits of the Earth, Inc.

The next day Tom was trimming the hedge at the front of the house when Skinner came by on his bicycle. At one time (before Billy came, of course) Skinner had practically worshipped Tom. He was two years younger than the others, and small and skinny as well; so they hadn't wanted him around. But Tom had said to let him stay — and that was when Tom's word had counted.

Skinner slowed down and finally stopped his bicycle near Tom. "Hi there, Chicken Man!" he said, giggling.

Tom looked at him with contempt. He knew perfectly well that if he made a dive for the little rat, Skinner would start howling as though he were being tortured to death.

When he didn't get a rise out of Tom, Skinner hesitated for a moment, trying to think of a new way to irritate him. "I don't see your goofy friend around today," he said at last. "Boy, you two sure make a good pair. You're a couple of real losers."

Tom lowered the hedge clippers for a moment and stared at his antagonist.

"Beat it, Skinner," he said coldly.

"Yeah, sure, talk tough," Skinner said a little uncertainly. "The Cobras will get you," he added. "We'll get both you and Andrew. Who does he think he is, anyhow? Billy even offered to make him vice-president of the Cobras and he turned it down. Boy, you can't get much dumber than that!"

Suddenly Tom vaulted over the hedge, grabbed Skinner off his bike and pulled him down into the ditch behind the hedge.

"What happened?" he demanded fiercely.

"You're hurting me! Get off or you'll be sorry, Tom!" Skinner whined.

"I'll *really* hurt you unless you tell me what happened," Tom said harshly. He had to know why Andrew hadn't joined the Cobras.

"When we picked him up he asked why you weren't there," Skinner muttered sulkily, "but Billy just said it was because you weren't invited. Then when we started fishing, he wouldn't fish. He went wandering around looking at rocks and stuff. Boy, is he weird. Ow! Hey, stop it!"

Tom had bounced a little on Skinner's stomach.

"What else happened?" he demanded.

"I was just gonna tell you," Skinner whined. "Then we had a barbecue and fried the fish and ate and stuff.

Billy stood up and said he had an announcement to make. His father even kept quiet because it was so important. Then Billy said how the Cobras needed guys with brains and how everybody knew that Andrew was loaded with brains — and said he could be vice-president in charge of strategy and public relations.

"Andrew said how nice it was of us to ask him to join. Afterwards Billy's father said he sounded just like an old man getting a citizen-of-the-year award. Boy was that funny, because Billy told me he just asked him because we'd be rid of him in a couple of months when he went back to school. Ow! Hey, let me alone!"

Savagely Tom dug his knee into Skinner's stomach and stuffed grass in his mouth. If his mother caught him, he'd really be in for it. But he didn't care.

"You're wrong, Skinner. You're all wrong!" he said fiercely. "Andrew acted like a human being. You jerks who call yourselves Cobras are the stupid ones. Isn't that right?"

Tom dug his knee in again.

"Yeah! Ow, stop it, Tom!" Skinner whimpered. "Billy'll get you! Ow! All right, we're the stupid ones."

"That's better," Tom said. "Now tell me what else happened."

"Well, on the way back Billy explained the rules to him. Y'know — a Cobra can't associate with a proven chicken and a Cobra has to be loyal to other Cobras. That jerk — ow! — I mean Andrew, asked why you weren't a member. So Billy told him. He found out all about what a rotten chicken you are — ow! Tom, stop it!"

"You asked for it," Tom said grimly. "What else happened?"

By now Skinner was crying. Once more Tom dug his knee in.

"Ow! You're gonna be sorry. Ow! Then Billy said he couldn't have anything to do with you. It's the rules. Ow! I didn't make the rules, Tom! Andrew didn't say nothin' for awhile and Billy's father said how vicious you were beatin' up Billy that time. For a minute Andrew still didn't say nothin', but then he finally said that we were all wrong."

"And what did Billy say?" Tom demanded.

"That you had had all kinds of time to pass the initiation and that you couldn't do it. That you were too much of a chicken to do it and that you were really weird. Even Mr. MacPherson said he didn't care to have his son, or even his son's friends, associating with a boy who was so mentally unstable. Ow! That's what he said. I didn't say it!

"And — and then he described how hurt Billy was when you beat him up and how a boy who was such a coward and then took out his frustrations by jumping someone from behind was not fit company for other children. Ow, Tom! Don't! Hey!"

"Go on," Tom said grimly.

"Andrew said he thought they were wrong. He said, 'I'm afraid you have some serious misconceptions about Tom, Mr. MacPherson. He suffers from claustrophobia, which is not cowardice.' That's exactly what he said. Then Mr. MacPherson told Andrew that he was just a boy and didn't know anything about it. Andrew said he had studied some psychology and that you were just afraid of closed-in spaces, probably because of a — of a — I can't remember the word. Something that happened when you were small. And then Billy interrupted and said if Andrew was going to be a Cobra he had to stay away from you."

"Then what?" Tom demanded.

"Then Andrew said, 'In that case I'm afraid I'll have to withdraw from the organization. I can't subscribe to a club with such a policy of ignorance.' Boy, you should have heard Mr. MacPherson light into him! He called him a smart alecky little know-it-all and said he needed the seat of his pants warmed up and that he'd tell Andrew's father so."

"What did Andrew do?"

"He just listened to it all and when Mr. MacPherson was through yelling at him he said that his father would support him in his decision and that he thought Mr. MacPherson was setting a disgraceful example for Billy and us.

"We were at Andrew's house by then. Mr. MacPherson just about dragged him into the house, he was so mad. I don't know what happened in the house, but he was even madder when he came out. Billy said something and he told him to shut up."

Tom sat back in amazement. He knew everything Skinner had said was true, even the big words. Everybody used to call Skinner "Parrot" because he picked up everything everybody said and could usually recite it letter perfect.

As Tom relaxed, Skinner suddenly heaved and pulled himself away. He ran for his bicycle and took off like a scared rabbit. "Chicken! Chicken! Chicken!" he screamed over his shoulder.

Tom just sat back on his heels and smiled. Andrew had refused to join because of him. Boy, what a goof! Suddenly Tom was ashamed of himself for the way he'd felt when people had seen him playing ball with Andrew. So what if he was different? It was because he was different that he liked Tom in spite of his being a chicken.

But Andrew had said he wasn't a chicken. That confused Tom. Of course he was a chicken. Why else would he be so scared of going into the Black Tunnel? Tom thought for a moment. Both his parents and Andrew had talked about claustrophobia, but the word had gone right over his head. He didn't know what it meant, but they seemed to.

Slowly Tom walked towards the house, puzzling over what they had said. He went into his father's den and got the big dictionary. It took him two or three tries to figure out the spelling, but finally he found it. The definition read simply, "a morbid dread of closed-in places."

Well, that was right enough, Tom thought grimly. He sighed, confused. Knowing what caused it and knowing that Andrew and his parents didn't think he was chicken only helped a bit. He still couldn't face the Black Tunnel, and he knew he would always secretly feel like a chicken until he did.

Just then there was a knock at the kitchen door. It was Andrew.

"Hi! Come on in," Tom said quickly. He wanted to thank his friend for sticking up for him, but he didn't know how to start. Andrew smiled shyly as he stepped into the kitchen.

Suddenly there was a yowl and a crash. Andrew was lying on the floor and Mitzit, all her fur on end, was hissing furiously at him from a corner. Tom started to laugh and the ice was broken. Awkwardly Andrew stood up.

"Do you think I hurt her?" he asked anxiously. "I didn't mean to walk on her. I just didn't see her."

"No, nothing's hurt but her dignity." He grinned. Then in a rush he said, "I hear you turned down an invitation to join the Cobras. Skinner told me a little while ago."

Andrew looked at him in surprise.

"Well, yes," he said. "I found they were much too narrow in their views. Childish is really the word."

"Yeah, I suppose so." Tom blushed. He didn't know how to say thanks, so he said simply, "Well, I'm glad. The other guys all belong and they won't hang around with anyone who doesn't. So — so do you want a coke or anything?"

They sat down at the kitchen table with their pop and things felt easy again. Amid opinions of the chances of their favourite baseball teams, Tom relaxed and began to feel better about himself. When his mother came into the kitchen to tell him she was driving to Hamilton to shop, he greeted her so cheerfully that she blinked at him in amazement. Tom just smiled.

"Say, Tom," Andrew said after Mrs. Kirby had left, "the reason I came over was to see if you wanted to help me sell my rocks at the flea market. It's hard for just one person because you can't go for lunch or anything. It's just on weekends and I'll give you a third of the profits. That is, if you want to. I mean you don't have to if you have other things you want to do on the weekends. I wouldn't mind, you know. But I thought maybe you'd like to."

Visions of a new ten-speed bicycle danced in front of Tom's eyes. "Wow, that would be great!" he said eagerly. "That is, if my parents don't mind. I'm sure they won't, though. What do we do? Just sit around and wait on people?"

Andrew grinned.

"Pretty well. But there's some work to be done getting stuff ready. We have to make displays and things. Most people don't bother, but I've noticed that the ones who go to the trouble of arranging their things so they look nice always sell more. We'll probably have to spend every Friday getting ready, if that's okay with you."

If Andrew had said every single day until midnight, Tom still wouldn't have hesitated. "Sure! I don't care. How much do you think we can make?" he demanded.

"I don't know. I'm hoping to make around five hundred over the summer, to pay for a rock-hunting trip down to Mexico next Easter."

"You mean we might take in five hundred dollars just for selling rocks?" Tom asked. The amount seemed incredible to him.

"No. I mean, I hope we make more. I just figure my share for around five hundred. I'd pay you half of the profits, Tom, but I figure I'll need a third to buy more geodes and other things like that for next summer. I'm figuring that we'll each take a third after expenses, and then I'll put the last third aside to buy things for next year. Maybe if we do okay we could expand into other things too." Andrew's eyes had begun to sparkle. "Maybe we could take orders from rockhounds for hard-to-find specimens. Especially Americans. I found out that more than half the American tourists in

Ontario come up through Niagara Falls. That means they have to go past us. Just think of all those people and how many might be interested in rocks!"

Tom wasn't sure about the abundance of rockhounds, but he knew that during summer weekends almost every second car on the Queen Elizabeth Way had American licence plates. And he figured most of the tourists would be looking for souvenirs.

"How about selling other things, too?" Tom asked. "Not everyone wants rocks and the idea is to make money. Maybe we can sell — I don't know — maybe those little collections of rocks for kids. And my mom's always making handicrafts and things. Maybe we could sell some of those. And fruit! When the cherries and peaches are ripe we could sell some of those too!"

Andrew looked at him dubiously. "I don't know," he said, wrinkling his forehead. "We don't want to get junky, and I don't know about anything except rocks. Maybe if we tied everything into a theme or something . . . but we don't want *too* much different stuff, do we?"

Tom thought about it for a minute and decided Andrew had a point.

"Not too much," he agreed. "But maybe if we just sell natural things — things that are from natural materials. My mother says that the best things come from natural materials."

"Yeah," Andrew agreed slowly. "That might do it. A

'fruits of the earth' type of thing."

"We could make a sign," Tom said eagerly, "with that on it."

"With what on it?"

"Fruits of the earth! We can be Fruits of the Earth, Incorporated!" He jumped up. "Tell me, sir," he said, pretending that he was holding a microphone in front of Andrew's face, "as president of the international company, Fruits of the Earth, Incorporated, can you give our viewers a prediction of the future?"

Andrew leaned back in the chair and hitched his thumbs under his arms as though they were suspenders. "Well," he said pompously, "as president I feel I can say this: the future looks fruitful. Positively fruitful."

Then they both laughed and pretended to box with each other. Mitzit, still crouching in the corner, looked on in feline disgust.

They talked about their plans for a while longer, but they couldn't make any decisions because they were both too excited to think straight. Finally Andrew looked at the kitchen clock and said he had to go.

"My mother's taking me over to the plaza at St. Catharines to get some new clothes. So I'll see you later."

"Say, can you come back and give me a hand convincing my parents?" Tom asked. "You always sound more logical than I do, so maybe you can convince them better. Can you come this evening?"

Andrew grinned. "Sure," he said. "After all, with the future of this international corporation hanging in the balance, it's the least I can do."

Tom laughed and gave him a shove out the door. Andrew climbed onto his bicycle and wobbled over the gravel of the driveway, then began to pedal down the road.

Watching him, Tom gleefully thought about having his own ten-speed.

6
Tornado!

The air outside had become uncomfortably hot and sticky. Slowly Tom walked back into the kitchen, still thinking about the new bicycle and the chances of really making a profit at the flea market. Absent-mindedly he made himself a peanut-butter-and-honey sandwich and sat on the corner of the table to eat it — and to try to think of things that would sell to tourists. Mitzit took a flying leap and landed beside him.

"You're nothing but a little beggar, Mitzit," Tom said, rubbing the back of the cat's neck. If his pet had one passion in life, it was peanut butter. "Well, what do *you* think of the whole idea?" he added.

"Meow," Mitzit replied reproachfully as yet another bite of sandwich went into Tom's mouth.

Tom grinned and broke a bit off for her. "Don't you know that cats don't like peanut butter?" he asked.

Delicately Mitzit took the piece from his fingers and began chewing, her eyes almost shut and the tip of her tail twitching in bliss. Chuckling, Tom gave her the last quarter of his sandwich, then put her on the floor and went outside.

He wandered slowly through the back yard, trying to get his mind working. It was like walking through a greenhouse, the air had become so hot and steamy. As he passed the flower beds he noticed that they needed to be watered. Even his mother's wild flowers were beginning to look wilted.

That was an idea! They could sell wild flowers to the tourists — not the delicate ones that would die, of course, but some of the tough plants that grew wild all over the Escarpment. Tom decided to go right away to look for some small enough for hanging planters. They would make fine souvenirs, and they wouldn't cost him a cent.

He had occasionally searched for flowers with his mother, so he knew where to look. The Escarpment was covered with sturdy, handsome plants — fringed gentians that Tom thought looked like roses; liverleafs that grew in thrusting clumps of delicate flowers and sculptured leaves; wild strawberries; ferns; and Tom's favourite, bleeding hearts. Most people called the small, pink, heart-shaped flowers squirrel corn, but Tom preferred the other name because to him they looked like hearts that had broken open.

Those would be good plants, Tom decided, because despite their deceptive daintiness they were tough. His mother referred to them as exotic weeds because they thrived and multiplied wherever there was a bit of dirt.

Tom hurried into the house, ate another sandwich, and wrote a note to tell his mother he was going for a ride up the Escarpment. Then he scouted around for some old bowls to use as planters. Fortunately for him, his mother was a saver. Down in the root cellar under the house she had stored hundreds of old jars and bowls.

He selected half a dozen different ones — two small goldfish bowls, an interesting looking jar, and three round, coloured-glass bowls. He dug his knapsack out of the shed to carry them in, then picked up a trowel and shoved that in too. With the knapsack safely over his shoulders, Tom pulled out his bike and started down the road.

It seemed like a long time since he had been up on the Escarpment. But instead of the usual fierce, empty feeling, Tom felt cheerful and content. He whistled under his breath, and thought of all his good plans.

He sniffed for the familiar smell of dust, but it wasn't there. Too much rain lately, he figured. Since it had been falling at night, it hadn't interfered with his days. But he'd heard on the radio that some of the farmers a little farther north were worried that the ground would be too wet for their crops to develop properly.

Well, the rain might be threatening the ground crops, but it was doing great things for the fruit in the region. He'd heard his father say that, barring a sudden dry spell or hail storm, they'd have a bumper fruit crop this year.

Tom pulled off the road where he could get a good view and looked down at the orchards that surrounded most of the houses. Here and there he could see tints of orangy red where the cherries were beginning to ripen. In another two or three weeks, at the latest, they would be ready to be picked. The peaches were still no more than hard, green, walnut-sized balls under the leaves. The last of the cherries would have been picked before the peaches would be ready to eat.

This summer the weather and the orchards were important to him. That fruit represented money to be coaxed from the tourists. He knew they'd gobble up all the fresh-picked, sun-warmed fruit he could offer them. Since his parents never had time to harvest all the fruit from their own trees, much of it went to the birds and the neighbours. If there was going to be a bumper crop, there would be enough for his mother's jams, the neighbours, and the tourists too. Even the birds would still do all right.

It was going to be a good summer.

Tom got back on his bicycle and began pedalling up the road again. The breeze, which had been steady and hot, became strong and gusty, sometimes pushing him up the hill, sometimes pressing him back. Under the erratic slaps of wind, the trees began tossing their branches more and more wildly.

Directly above, the sky was still a pure, serene blue, but between the sweeping tree branches and the flashing silver undersides of the leaves, Tom saw banks of clouds pressing down over the lake a few miles away. He watched the clouds for a few minutes, debating whether to give up the search and go home or to go on and risk a wetting.

He decided to go on. The wind gave him a sense of urgency and he pedalled furiously. Small sounds began to echo through the air as the wind and the pressure from the lowering clouds changed and distorted them.

Tom felt a surge of elation. He loved storms: the wild clapping of thunder and the erratic flashing of lightning both excited and frightened him. And then afterwards everything would be quiet and serene, as though the world had just been re-created.

He reached the top of the Escarpment; the sun was still shining up there and the sounds were normal. Tom stopped at the lookout and gazed at the flat land below, and at the shadowed, slate-grey lake beyond. Already he could see flashes of lightning over the lake, hear the slow, distant roll of thunder. But there was no point in heading back — the storm might not even hit the top of the Escarpment. Besides, down in the gorge he would probably be protected from the worst of it. His decision made, he rode on past the mill, left his bicycle in the empty field, then clambered and swung his way down the gorge.

Tom had never really paid much attention to the plants growing in the gorge, but now that he was looking closely at them, he saw how beautiful most of them were — as green and lush as any in a greenhouse, without the man-made order imposed by a gardener. They tumbled and spilled over each other, sprouting crazily out of little cracks in the rock walls, all leaning sideways and yearning upwards to the bright sunlight that filtered through the thick leaves of the trees.

Only some of the plants had flowers. Most of them were beautiful, but their appeal lay in the unusual shapes of the leaves. One had a spidery sprawl of leaves all tangled in attractive profusion; and one grew in a tough little bundle with large self-contained leaves on the outside and progressively smaller ones in the centre. When Tom carefully spread the outer leaves apart, he could see tiny, perfect ones forming in the heart of the plant, still the same shape and proportions but just a slightly paler tint of green. There were several kinds of ferns — some with long, delicate fronds and others with stubbier, thicker fronds like green lace ruffles.

"Oh boy, are we going to make a mint," Tom muttered to himself as he quickly unpacked his knapsack. Making a quick survey of the area, he decided to transplant one sample of each of the most attractive plants. That way they could see which ones were tough enough to sell.

It took a long time to dig each one up. When Tom

had helped his mother gather the ones for her garden, she had told him that the secret of transplanting a wild plant was to try to dig up all of its roots and plant it quickly without letting any of the dirt fall off. Those that grew in clusters weren't too difficult because they were small plants with small roots. But the ground was very rocky. After struggling for some minutes to dig one up, Tom decided to move farther down the gorge where the earth might be softer.

He was so intent on his search for plants that small changes in the feel of the air and in the echoes of sounds made no impression on him. He had just transplanted a tiny fern when a tingling feeling in the back of his neck suddenly snapped him into awareness. Quickly he looked around, sniffed the air, looked at the sky. Above him, the last patch of blue disappeared, swallowed by a purple-black bank of clouds.

Everywhere was silence — a terrible, waiting silence. The leaves on the trees hung limp. There was no sound of birds.

Tom felt a shiver run down his spine. He had never seen clouds as heavy and as black as these. In all the years he had lived beside the Escarpment, he had never felt this kind of stillness. He fought down a surge of panic. This was going to be some storm! Was there time to get home? He had walked quite a way down the gorge, and if the storm hit while he was trying to get up the cliff . . .

The decision was made for him when raindrops splattered and the wind began to gust. Frantically Tom gathered up his knapsack, bowls and plants and hurried towards the head of the gorge, where the waterfall and the two cliff sides formed a semi-sheltered basin. If it were a really bad storm, he could take refuge inside the Black Tunnel.

Tom looked up at the wild sky and swallowed.

By the time he had scrambled to the mouth of the Tunnel, he knew this was not an ordinary storm. The wind had risen wildly, wailing and screaming through the trees. The rain was lashing his face and bare arms like cold chips of stone driven before the wind. Bits of ice began to mingle with the rain, tearing plants and ricocheting off tree trunks, bruising his body. He had to have shelter.

Suddenly there was an ear-splitting crack overhead. Tom ran. A huge branch had been torn off one tree and flung wildly against another. It dropped where Tom had been standing.

There could be no hesitation. The wind was rising even more, buffeting and pushing him fiercely. He had to get out of it, away from the trees, away from the fury of the storm.

Tom reached the mouth of the Tunnel. It did not look like a haven. It sweated and dripped and moaned with each gust of wind. But there was no other place.

From ghosties and ghoulies
And long-legged beasties
And things that go bump in the night,
Good Lord deliver me!

Tom said the rhyme half seriously, half jokingly, to give himself courage. His mother had heard the prayer from a Scottish friend and had whispered it to him comfortingly when he was small and could not bear to be alone in the dark.

With the roar of the wind and the howling of the tortured trees behind him, Tom moved a bit farther into the Tunnel. There was a small niche in the wall a little way back from the entrance, with a rough ledge of stone a short distance off the ground. It was damp, but it was a place to sit with his back against the wall. Positioned there, his feet propped up on a stone just out of the cold water covering the bottom of the Tunnel, he could watch both the storm and the waiting blackness of the Tunnel.

He tried to ignore the Tunnel and concentrated on the storm. The wind shrieked wildly and the rain came down in sheets; the trees tossed in agony; limbs were torn away willy-nilly and hurled into the stream, or smashed against the cliff walls. The sky was a mass of churning blackness, thick and deep and covering everything.

The madness carried on and on, until Tom began to think that it would never end, that he would crouch shivering in the Tunnel forever. Then suddenly there was silence. The wind dropped. The trees hung limp and beaten.

His feet numb, Tom crept out of the Tunnel. Maybe it was over and he could go home. But when he looked up and saw the clouds still churning, more wildly than ever, he knew it wasn't over.

"It's just starting," he whispered to himself. He was afraid. Not the kind of dread he had of the Tunnel, but a primitive fear of a storm he knew could kill him if he were caught in it.

The wind began again, a low, sighing, groaning sound. Tom stood and watched, fascinated but afraid, unwilling to move. The gale grew wilder, louder, until above him was a strange howling roar. Tom looked up at the clouds. A long black funnel was pulling to the ground, reeling drunkenly.

A tornado!

"They don't have tornadoes here," Tom whispered.

Terrified, he dived back into the Tunnel. Shivering, he pressed his back against the rock and watched in horror.

The tornado skipped back and forth, swaying and twisting madly across the top of the Escarpment. The wind howled. The tornado never dipped into the gorge but crossed it four times, each time swirling debris and tree limbs everywhere. Finally it veered away, lurching down the gorge, still spewing twisted wreckage along its path.

Once again Tom crept out of the Tunnel. Fearfully he gazed after the black funnel. It was sweeping over the spot where he had climbed down the cliff! If he had tried to make it home during the calm , . .

At last the tornado moved out of sight. Tom could still hear the roar in the distance, but it began to grow fainter. He looked up. The churning black clouds had moved off, leaving more normal, slate-coloured ones.

The storm was over.

7
Making plans

With a sigh of relief Tom walked into the gorge to see
what damage the tornado had done.

Everywhere huge limbs lay at odd angles — or
dangled from strangely tough pieces of bark still
attached to the trees. The river was loaded with wood,
branches, and everything else the storm had dumped.
Already it was swelling from the water that had poured
into it. Overhead, the sky was still bleak, but at least it
was a normal storm colour.

Twice on the way down the gorge Tom had to
scramble over trees that had been uprooted and lay
across the path. It occurred to him that in a few years
they would be soft, damp and rotting, like the ones he
had always taken for granted. All the smaller vines on
the cliff face had been ripped away from the rock, but
the father vine he used for climbing still clung there —
battered, but very tough. Tom grinned. It felt like an old
friend, too tough and snarly to be seriously disturbed by

anything as trivial as a tornado.

Slowly and carefully Tom picked his way to the top of the cliff. A tree, uprooted from the field above, had slid into the gorge so that it lay upside down at the foot of the path, leaning against the cliff, but with its upper branches trailing in the water of the swelling stream. Tom used the massive trunk for support as he scrambled up the cliff side.

The field where he had left his bike just a few hours before had completely changed. Trees had been toppled and dragged yards away from their rooting places. Most of the wild grass and bushes were flattened and torn — although in some places they seemed totally untouched.

Tom rubbed his hand through his hair. He had never imagined anything like this. And what about his bicycle? He looked around anxiously, but could see neither the bush where he had hidden it nor the bicycle itself.

Not knowing what else to do, Tom began scouting around the field, swearing under his breath as he thought of the long walk home. He wondered if his parents had returned yet, and if they were worried about him.

"Come on," he said to himself in exasperation. "It's got to be here somewhere."

Finally he found it, lying upside down in a small gully about sixty metres away, and all tangled with broken branches. It took twenty minutes to haul the bicycle free of the snarled branches, and then the results were discouraging.

"It's going to be a long walk," Tom muttered as he surveyed the twisted frame.

The front wheel was ruined — most of the spokes gone and the frame bent. The handlebars were bent too, though not as much. The back end didn't look too bad, but the reflector was smashed and the wheel had lost a couple of spokes.

Ruefully he calculated how long it would take him to fix it. His dad would probably help him, and pay for a new front wheel so it would be usable again. But it would never be as good as it was before.

Tom settled the plants and the knapsack into the carrier and started walking, pushing the bike as he went and thinking about how long it would take him to save for a ten-speed. "Boy, I could sure use one now," he said in exasperation as he struggled with the bent handlebars.

But when he reached the road, he forgot about the bicycle. Everything the tornado had touched had been pulled down or torn off, and scattered wildly. The destruction within the relatively sheltered gorge was nothing compared to the damage on the exposed Escarpment.

Hydro poles leaned drunkenly, and some had toppled over altogether. Trees had crashed through live wires.

The old barns and sheds that had dotted the area had disappeared, except for an odd corner post sticking bleakly upright amid a tangle of boards or just a patch of bare ground. Branches and torn-up fences from vineyards were everywhere.

"Wow," Tom said as he walked along viewing the wreckage. He saw Mr. Piers glumly surveying a branch that had shot through one of the glass windows of the mill. Tom leaned his bike against a fence post and walked over to talk to him.

"Much damage?" he asked.

"Enough," Mr. Piers said sourly. "I never thought I'd see a tornado around here, that's for damn sure! My house is all right, except for a few shingles ripped off. But this glass here" — he gestured emphatically — "this glass has been in this window as long as I can remember. It's not like the glass they have now. Don't know where I can get it replaced or even who'll pay for it. The Parks Board spends next to nothing to keep these museums up, but they sure kick if they look shabby."

He looked around again. "It's a damn shame. People think I'm crazy the way I look after the place, but my great grandfather built it and I'm proud of it. Now I have to chase kids off because I can't keep the place on the money allotted for upkeep if they start messing around."

He glanced sharply at Tom. "What are you doing here? You weren't caught in the storm, were you?"

Suddenly he noticed Tom's bike. "Are you all right, boy?"

For an instant Tom had thought Mr. Piers was going to toss him off the property.

"I was down in the gorge collecting plant samples," he answered. "It wasn't as bad down there and I went into one of the tunnels when the storm hit. Boy that tornado was really something! I could see it skipping back and forth across the top of the gorge. Was I ever scared!"

For the first time, Mr. Piers smiled almost cheerfully. "Plants, eh? Well, the gorge is a good place for botany, I guess. You know, I don't mind telling you that when I saw that tornado forming I was pretty damn scared myself, and I had a strong cellar to hide in!"

They chatted amicably about the storm for a few more minutes. Then Tom remembered his parents would probably be home and worrying by now; so he started back towards the road.

"Hey!" Mr. Piers called after him suddenly. "Keep an eye on those tunnels. With all this rain they'll probably be draining the reservoir, and if you get caught in one when you're grubbing around for your plants, you'll be in pretty bad shape. I should hear when they're going to do it, so I'll let you know. Wouldn't want one of the decent kids around here washed downstream, would we?" he called cheerfully.

"Thanks, Mr. Piers," Tom shouted. He grinned as he

shoved his bicycle along the road. Somehow Mr. Piers had decided he was all right. Typical of adults to like you for something dumb like collecting plants or being caught in a storm!

As Tom walked along the highway he saw signs everywhere of the tornado's passing. Most of the vineyards had had some of their wire trellises ripped up. Down one of the side roads he could see a group of people standing around a frame house that had lost its roof.

He was beginning to feel tired when he spotted his parents' car slowly approaching along the debris-strewn road.

"Tom!" his mother called as she hurried out of the car. "Are you all right? Oh, Tom, we were so worried about you."

"I'm okay," he answered, pushing his bike over to the car. "I sat the storm out in one of the tunnels down in the gorge. It didn't do my bike much good though."

Tom's father examined the bicycle and shook his head. Tom hoped he was going to say something like "I guess we'll have to buy you a new one. Would you like a ten speed?" But instead he said what Tom had expected.

"It's going to take a bit of fixing, but it should be all right. How many times have I told you not to leave your bike out during tornadoes," he added with a grin.

"Gee, Dad, I'm sorry," Tom said in mock repentance. "I won't do it again, honest." He recalled his feelings during the storm and added, "In fact, that's a promise!"

They loaded the bike into the trunk and started for home. On the way, Tom told them about Andrew's plans for opening a booth at the flea market and showed them the plants he had found. As casually as he could, he mentioned how much he wanted a new ten-speed.

"We'll have to talk to Andrew and see what he has planned before we say yes or no," his mother said seriously. "We wouldn't want you to commit yourself to something that isn't possible. But if Andrew has it as well organized as you think he does, and if he's already rented the space for the booth, I can't see why not."

His father nodded in agreement. "Sounds like a good idea to me. If you're so keen to work and earn money, I can't see how it would hurt."

Tom leaned back against the seat and smiled. Things were shaping up just fine. Vaguely, and then with a slight sense of shock, he remembered that he had actually spent more than an hour in the mouth of the Tunnel. It sure wasn't much, he thought grimly, but after all, he had to start somewhere.

At about eight o'clock that evening Andrew arrived at the kitchen door. He was loaded down with a knapsack full of carefully wrapped rock specimens and several sheets of paper covered with scrawly writing and lopsided drawings.

"Hi, Tom," he said cheerfully. "I brought all my plans and a few specimens. A complete presentation is always important."

Tom grinned.

"Mom and Dad are in the living room reading," he said. He led the way and Andrew pushed awkwardly through the swinging door after him.

"Evening, Mr. and Mrs. Kirby," Andrew said casually, with a cheerful grin. Again Tom marvelled at Andrew's ease with adults. He always treated them as though they were on the same level as himself. But then, Tom acknowledged to himself, with his brains maybe they were.

The two boys spread everything out on the floor in front of Tom's parents. Quickly Andrew arranged the rocks into groups.

"These," he said, pointing to the cut and polished geodes, "we plan to sell as ornamental bookends. I have some very colourful, though not particularly good, samples of quartz which can also be used for bookends — or coffee table conversation pieces."

Tom picked up a large piece of glimmering white quartz, marbled through with pink. "What's wrong with this?" he asked.

"The crystals are too small and the impurity that makes the pink colour is too common to make it worth anything much as a geological sample," Andrew explained, running the tips of his long fingers over its surface.

"But it's beautiful," Tom's mother exclaimed. "I wouldn't mind having bookends made from that for the glass coffee table I want to buy."

Andrew smiled. "Exactly," he said. "It didn't cost me much because I bought it as a rock sample. But it is very pretty, so we should be able to sell it to tourists at a good profit. At least to any tourists who aren't interested in minerals," he added with a trace of resignation.

"You sound as if all you want are people who collect rocks," Tom grinned. "They'll know too much about them to buy anything we have to offer."

"Oh no, Tom," Andrew exclaimed. "Of course I'll have some excellent specimens available, too, for anyone interested in geology. Most of them I found myself, so we'll get pure profit on them. I had to buy some, but we can still make about fifty percent on those."

"Well, that's sure going to be your department," Tom said ruefully. "What do you think, Mom and Dad? Does it seem like a good idea to you?" Exchanging glances, he and Andrew held their breath. At last Tom's father sat back in his chair and smiled at them.

"Sounds good to me," he said. "I don't know if you'll make the money you think you will, because there are a lot of people competing madly to get the tourists' souvenir business. But the experience won't hurt you, and you'll probably break even at least."

Tom and Andrew smiled in relief.

"Great!" Tom said. "The first sale is next Saturday, so we're going to have to hustle to get ready."

Andrew nodded. "Are you any good at lettering, Tom?" he asked anxiously. "I'm not, and we'll have to make a sign for the booth and price tags for things, and little explanation signs. No one would look twice at the stuff if I made them," he added.

Tom nodded. "Sure," he said, "let's go up to my room and get started." If Andrew really did need him, he would honestly earn his share of the profits.

Tom's father stood up and switched on the television set. "If you need a place to work," he suggested, "you can use my den — so long as you clean it up."

"Sure thing, Dad," Tom said, trying to sound casual. With his father offering the use of his den, there was no doubt that his parents had been thoroughly impressed with Fruits of the Earth, Incorporated.

It didn't take long to get organized. Andrew had sketches of the booth he had rented, and his notations on how much they had to sell to break even.

Tom showed him the plants he had dug up — only one had wilted — and then they spent several minutes re-figuring profits based on how much merchandise they would have available over the summer. Next they started plans for the booth's layout.

"Should we put everything in sections, or should we

mingle it?" Tom asked.

"Let's try it with the samples we have here," Andrew suggested.

It took them an hour to reach an arrangement they both liked. At Tom's suggestion Andrew jotted their ideas down on their sketches so they would have something to refer to later. They worked until after nine-thirty, then regretfully Andrew sat back in his chair.

"I'd better get going," he said. "I told my parents I'd be home around ten."

"We sure have a lot more work to do," Tom remarked as he turned over the pages of plans. "We'll have to spend at least a day pricing things and making tags for them. And we'll need another day for collecting plants. I want to learn how to do the fancy knot-tying my mother does so I can make hanging plant-holders."

"Is that macramé?" Andrew rubbed his forehead wearily. "I saw some of those in the craft shop at the plaza this morning. They were selling just the string part for anywhere from two to twenty dollars, depending on how fancy they were, of course. That would really add up if the tourists bought ours as fast as they were selling in the shop."

"Well, it's worth learning then," Tom said. "I don't suppose you'd be any good at it, would you?"

"With these magic fingers" — Andrew held up his

lanky hands — "I can tangle anything with the speed of light. It's the untangle part I haven't mastered."

They laughed and joked while they cleaned up. For the first time in ages Tom felt as though he was really sharing something with someone. And then he thought of the others.

"Boy," he said with relish, "the Cobras are going to turn green when they see the money we're going to make."

Andrew smiled slightly and glanced at Tom, but didn't say anything.

"Don't you think so?" Tom persisted.

"Yeah," Andrew agreed slowly. "But I don't think that crowd will realize how much work and organization we'll have to put into it. Probably they'll never think of the money we're risking — because we do have to make enough to cover our expenses." He hesitated for a minute. "You know that guy Billy — I don't trust him. There's a guy like that at my school. He wants everything but he won't work for it. If he can't bully someone into handing over what he wants, he tries to find some way to wreck it. I'm afraid Billy might act like that, especially because I lost my temper and wouldn't join the Cobras. So I don't think we should say anything to them about what we're doing, especially if it's a success."

"Aw, what can he do?" Tom protested. "You're not scared of him, are you?"

Andrew looked startled. "No, of course not," he said firmly. "But I think we'd be very foolish to ask for trouble. Don't you?"

Tom hesitated. "Yeah, I suppose so," he finally said, reluctantly. Part of his pleasure had been in knowing he was one up on Billy. A little guiltily he realized he hadn't been thinking much about the work or the risk either — or the money it cost.

"But I still don't see what Billy could do," he repeated. "After all, if we don't tell anyone what we're doing, no one will know where to come and buy what we've got. Of course we don't have to rub it in," he added.

Andrew smiled. "I guess you're right. I'm anxious because I've had so many run-ins with that other guy at my school. And because I usually lose," he added ruefully. "I'm not anxious to start the same kind of feud here at home."

"I'm not scared of Billy," Tom boasted. "We can handle him and any of the Cobras. You'll see."

"I hope not," Andrew remarked dryly as he put on his coat to go home.

8
Who wants to be like Billy?

During the next few days Tom and Andrew spent all their time getting ready for the flea market on Saturday. For two days straight it rained — a heavy, drizzly downpour under slate-grey skies. For the first time in his life Tom worried frantically about the weather. What if they couldn't get to the gorge to collect plants? Or what if the tourists stayed home and he and Andrew went broke?

Because he still felt guilty about not realizing how much things were costing, Tom took out his own savings — almost twenty dollars — and used it to buy some things they still needed for the sale. Andrew had offered to pay for everything, but Tom figured it wouldn't be fair. If the sale was a success, Tom would get a full share of the profits. If it was a flop Andrew would have been the only one to lose.

The two of them spent an afternoon in St. Catharines buying blank price tags, different coloured felt-tipped pens, macramé twine, receipt books, and all the other things they needed. It had taken Tom a year and a half to save the twenty dollars, but it disappeared in less than an hour and a half.

"How does it feel to be a full-fledged business man?" Andrew asked with a grin.

Tom grimaced as he counted what was left of his savings. "Poor!" he said wryly. "I have seventy-eight cents left. Let's blow the bundle and buy ice cream cones."

As they waited for the bus and ate their ice cream, Andrew rechecked everything they had purchased. "We should be all ready for those souvenir-hungry tourists," he remarked with satisfaction.

"Yeah," Tom agreed gloomily as he stared out the window at the non-stop rain, "providing the tourists come in the rain — *and* if we can get everything done on time."

But despite Tom's fears and the rain, everything was ready by seven-thirty on Friday night, and the radio forecast indicated a beautiful, warm weekend.

Tom and Andrew were drinking pop on the steps of the pharmacy, enjoying the feel of a finished job and a couple of hours in which there was absolutely nothing they had to do. The night was warm, although a fresh breeze was blowing.

"Boy, it sure feels nice knowing that everything's done," Tom remarked.

"Uh-huh," Andrew answered absently. "Will you look at those stars? Sometimes I think I should study astronomy at university, instead of geology. What do you think, Tom?"

"I think you're nuts," Tom replied with a grin. "Completely and totally split in the noggin."

Andrew made a face, then tilted back his head and let the rest of the pop trickle down his throat. Dispassionately Tom watched his friend's Adam's apple slide up and down his throat as he swallowed.

"Think we'll make much?" he asked for the hundredth time. They both chuckled.

"You know," Tom added, "I've been thinking. We should make up a list of everything we've got, and whenever we sell something, put a tick beside that item. That way we'll know what we need to stock up on and what doesn't seem to sell well."

"Good idea," Andrew said, pulling his rangy body to his feet. "I'll get some paper and we can do it now."

He disappeared into the pharmacy. Tom leaned back and looked down the road. His body stiffened. Billy and all the other guys were wheeling their bicycles towards the pharmacy.

"Well," Billy said with a sneer twisting his face, "if it isn't Chicken Man. I thought they would have taken you to the butcher's by now. But I guess you still run too fast for them to catch you, eh, chicky?"

Billy looked at the others and they snickered in

appreciation. Like puppets, Tom thought.

"Take off, why don't you?" he snarled. "I have work to do."

"What kind of work is that?" Billy taunted. "They got you holding the steps down in case the wind blows them away? Is that it, Chicken Man?"

The others were roaring with laughter when Andrew came out again. He grimaced when he saw the Cobras, hesitated, then obviously decided to ignore them.

"My dad's loaded most of the stuff in the car," he said quietly to Tom. "The sign and a few other things are still in the shed because we'll have to hold them in our laps on the way. We had better start our lists, I guess."

"Well, look who's here too," Billy remarked in a carrying voice. "Chicken Man's faithful jerk, the String-Bean Brain."

"Look, Billy," Tom said hotly, "either you take off or we'll send you crying home to your mother — again!"

Tom and Billy glared at each other. Tom guessed the Cobras didn't know their leader had cried like a baby the time Tom had beat him up. Knowing he could humiliate Billy, if only for a minute, pleased him.

Andrew put his hand on Tom's arm. "We should get to work on this,'" he said, stammering slightly. "We won't make our first million if we don't have everything ready for the flea market."

"Yeah," Tom agreed. He glared another second at

Billy, then nonchalantly started listing things on the paper.

"We'll have to make big columns for the things we sell a lot of," he said.

Andrew nodded.

Billy had been staring uncertainly at them. Suddenly he started to laugh. "You mean you two losers have got a booth at the flea market?" he hooted. "Boy! That should be good for a laugh."

"Oh yeah?" Tom shouted, jumping to his feet. "While you jerks are goofing off I'll be making the money for a racing bicycle and Andrew will be making reservations for a trip to Mexico."

"You won't make a cent," Billy jeered.

"You're too dumb, Chicken Man," Skinner giggled.

The Cobras, as though to a drilled signal, began shouting and jeering and yelling insults. Furiously Tom took a swing at Billy, who dodged it. Andrew jumped up and grabbed Tom.

"Look, why let these jerks bother you? We have things to do. Let's get another pop and go into the back of the store."

Tom hesitated. If only he could get at Billy . . .

"C'mon!" Andrew urged.

"All right," Tom finally agreed. There were too many of them to fight by himself. And besides, they did have to get the list done.

"So long, losers," he called mockingly over his shoulder.

"Don't think you're going to get anywhere," Billy returned viciously, "because I personally guarantee that you won't!"

"Sure!" Tom shouted derisively as the pharmacy door swung behind them.

"Boy, those guys bug me!" he said hotly to Andrew when they had settled into the back room to work. "Would I ever like to get even with them. Especially that fat-faced baby who calls himself the president."

"Lay off, Tom," Andrew said with a hint of annoyance in his voice, "or else we may really get into trouble. As far as I'm concerned, they aren't worth getting upset about."

He spread the papers determinedly on the desk and picked up a pen.

"Yeah, but — " Tom faltered. He wanted to say that it was different for Andrew, that he didn't have a score to settle with Billy. But when he looked at his friend's determined face, he hesitated. Suddenly he felt foolish and a little childish. Uncertainly he waited for Andrew to say something, but he just stared at the list as though Tom wasn't even there.

"I suppose you're right," Tom said grudgingly. "Billy's managed to make things rough for me ever since he moved here and I hate him. But even if I could get back at him, I suppose I probably wouldn't."

Andrew smiled gratefully at Tom and his bony shoulders relaxed. Suddenly he was eager and shy again.

"Yeah," he said. "The only way to get back at Billy would be to do the things he does, and then we'd be just like the Cobras. I mean, you know what's best for you, Tom, and I wasn't around in the winter — but who wants to be someone like Billy?"

Tom laughed with a touch of relief. "I hadn't thought of it that way. That would be the absolute pits of everything!"

Once good feelings were restored, it didn't take long to make up their lists. But they spent a long while talking over everything that might happen during their sale.

"Well, we'll see what happens tomorrow," Tom said as he got up to go home.

Andrew walked him to the street, then waved goodbye. Tom climbed onto his bicycle and started towards home.

Just on the other side of the pharmacy was an overgrown lot filled with lilac and honeysuckle bushes. As Tom pedalled by, a gleam of something shiny deep in the bushes caught his eye. He slowed down and tried to peer through the dense growth. It was too dark and the bushes were too thick to see anything. For a moment Tom hesitated, then he slipped off his bike and forced his way along a small path into the bushes.

It took only a moment to find out what the gleam had

been — a bit of moonlight glinting off the handlebars of Billy's bicycle. Tom looked around carefully. There were several more bikes hidden, but none of the Cobras were anywhere to be seen.

Well, this would sure be a chance to get even, Tom thought gleefully. They were probably off doing something exciting, thinking they were so great. But with all the air let out of their tires, the Cobras would have a long walk home.

Quickly he found a pebble the right size and knelt to let the air out of the valves. Then he hesitated. This was the kind of thing Billy would do. No, Billy would be more likely to go all the way and punch holes in the tires — providing, of course, it was Tom's bicycle.

But he didn't want to be like Billy. Tom opened his hand and dropped the pebble. He stood up and slowly walked back to the road. He could feel the fresh warm breeze blowing gently around his head and arms, and he could hear all the small night sounds. For a moment he felt very lonely. But he also felt good, in a shivery, strange sort of way.

That night as he got ready for bed, Tom made a little change in his ritual. He turned off his light before he crawled safely under the covers. Then slowly, purposefully, he walked to the other side of the bed and settled himself in without allowing a hint of panic to flicker in his mind.

"Funny," he said with a yawn to Mitzit as she curled

up beside him. "Billy will never know I could have got even on him and didn't . . . I wonder if he turns his light out before or after he gets into bed."

* * *

When the alarm rang the next morning, the sun was streaming into his room. Tom jumped out of bed and looked through the window at the blue, blue sky. No rain today.

We'll make our fortunes for sure, he thought happily. He could just see it. There would be tourists everywhere and they'd all come over to see what was for sale under the sign *Fruits of the Earth*.

It was a terrific sign, the result of pooling their ideas. Andrew had suggested the best design and style for the letters, even though he couldn't draw himself. But Tom had thought of using an old piece of barn board — there were enough of them lying around on the Escarpment after the tornado.

Just thinking about the sign made Tom feel good. They had printed *Fruits of the Earth* in a deep blue colour, using an angular style of printing they had found in a book about lettering they had borrowed from the library. Then in the corners they had drawn designs of brightly-coloured plants and fruit, and not too bad a rendition of a six-sided quartz crystal. It had taken a whole day to make it, but it was worth it. Both sets of parents had admired it.

Tom's mother was in the kitchen, dressed in her housecoat, when he clattered downstairs. "I thought I had better get a good breakfast into you before you started on your first million," she said with a sleepy smile.

Tom grinned and began helping her. He chattered enthusiastically about how well everything would go and she murmured drowsy replies. Saturday was usually her sleep-in morning.

Before long Tom was on his bicycle heading towards Andrew's house. Glancing quickly at his wrist watch, he saw it was just after eight. Right on time. Since the flea market opened for business at ten, they had decided to meet at eight-thirty so they would have lots of time to set up their booth. Tom had some strong screw-in hooks in his pocket in case there was nothing on the overhead bar of the booth for hanging their sign.

The wind was cool but the sun was bright and warm. There still wasn't much of a smell of dust, Tom noticed — it had rained again during the night. They would have to empty the reservoir a bit for sure now.

It was twenty-eight minutes past eight by Tom's watch when he reached Andrew's house. He propped his bicycle up at the side, raced around the corner and crashed into Andrew, who had come bounding down the steps of the front porch. Both of them landed on the ground.

"Gee, Tom, I didn't see you," Andrew apologized quickly.

"Well, I didn't see you either." Tom laughed and pulled his friend to his feet. "You all set?"

"Yeah, I was just going to get the stuff out of the shed."

Just as they started towards the shed at the back, Mr. MacDonald came out through the back door. "Beautiful morning, eh? I'll help you boys load up," he said cheerfully. Like Andrew, he was tall and lanky.

Andrew pulled open the shed door and Tom switched on the overhead light. Then they stood motionless, gaping.

"Oh, no!" Andrew exclaimed.

"What the hell — " Mr. MacDonald exploded.

Tom didn't say anything because for an instant he was afraid he was going to cry.

The shed was a mess. The carefully potted plants had been dumped onto the floor; the cord Tom had spent hours tying into intricate knots had been tied into even more intricate tangles; boxes of rock samples had been dumped into the spilled dirt from the plants; paint had been poured over everything.

And their beautiful sign had been smashed. The wood was split down the grain, and smeared across their careful printing, large messy letters spelled the one word — *COBRAS.*

9
End of the Cobras

Tom, Andrew and Mr. MacDonald stared at the ruin of the boys' careful work.

"Well, what do we do now?" Andrew asked glumly as he poked with his foot at the ruined rock samples.

"I'll kill Billy!" Tom choked furiously. "He's wrecked everything on purpose. I hate those Cobras!"

"Do you boys know who did this?" Mr. MacDonald asked sharply. "Because this is a lot more than a harmless prank and I intend to treat it as such."

"What do you mean, Dad?"

"Whoever did this has broken the law," Mr. Mac-Donald replied grimly as he examined some of the damage. "They have trespassed on private property, broken into a building and wantonly destroyed your belongings. The Cobras are that gang of boys who hang around the store sometimes, aren't they?" he asked. "The ones who were giving you a hard time last night? I was going to chase them off, but I figure you're old enough to fight your own battles. And," he added angrily, "they are certainly old enough to be fully responsible for this."

"But what can we do?" Tom asked helplessly as he picked up a wilted fern.

"Well, I guess we had better salvage what we can," Mr. MacDonald replied. "We'll load it in the car with the other stuff and get you to the flea market."

"Yeah, there's no point standing around looking at this mess," Andrew agreed. "At least we still have the stock in the car."

"That stuff won't look nearly as good by itself," Tom said glumly. All he felt like doing was going home and getting back into bed. Billy would probably always manage to ruin his plans, and as far as he was concerned right now, it was hardly worth fighting him. Tom sat down on a box and sullenly stubbed his toe in the spilled dirt.

Andrew looked at him. "You don't think we should just give up, do you, Tom?" he asked anxiously. "I mean, you don't want to call off the partnership, do you?"

"No." Reluctantly Tom stood up. "I guess we can manage with the stuff in the car. But I'd sure like to get back at Billy," he added viciously when his eyes lit again on the smashed sign. For a moment he bitterly regretted not having slashed the Cobras' tires the night before when he had had the chance. But he still didn't want to be like Billy.

"Well, we'll see what can be done," Mr. MacDonald said, a trace of grimness still in his voice. "I'll drive you boys to the market and see what I can do while you're gone."

The drive was quieter than Tom would have thought possible the night before. But when they arrived and started to take stock of what they had left to sell, it wasn't as bad as he and Andrew had thought. They still had some plants and all of the more valuable rocks, plus two or three of the small rock collections for children that Andrew had carefully prepared. But the one thing they both felt they couldn't replace was the sign.

The parking lot was full of busy people. The sale was being held in an old building — long, rough and dusty. It had probably once served as a farm building of some sort. This flea market had the advantage of being under a roof in case of rain, and it could be seen from the highway. It was illegal to put signs on the Queen Elizabeth Way, but the big sign that had been erected on the roof of the building was easily visible from a good distance down the highway.

Because of the depletion of their wares and their careful planning beforehand, Tom and Andrew had their booth arranged almost half an hour before the doors would be opened to customers. Tom finished placing the carefully hand-printed cards beside the rocks and plants and stood back to see the effect.

"Doesn't look half bad," Andrew said. "The sign would have really made it something special, though."

"We'll have to make another sign next week," Tom said. "How about a trip up the Escarpment on Monday or Tuesday to get another board and collect a few more plants?"

"Sure," Andrew agreed. "Let's go take a look at the other booths."

They spent the next half hour wandering around and examining the other goods offered for sale. Tom felt a lot better after that, because even without the sign their booth was one of the most attractive in the building.

There was quite a variety of goods being offered. Most people had rented booths for the season, as Tom and Andrew had, and sold goods not normally available in stores — weaving, wood carving, all kinds of needlework, and even hand-blown glass. A few other booths were rented only for the day or for the weekend, by people just interested in clearing out their cellars and attics. Old lampshades, cheap pictures, some used bottles and the like — these were the things they were selling. Usually they made only token attempts at attractive displays. Most of the goods simply lay in disorganized piles.

"I can't imagine anyone buying any of that junk," Tom said after examining one such pile.

"You'd be surprised. Most of it is dirt cheap, and people will buy the goofiest things if they're cheap enough."

"Maybe," Tom said doubtfully as they strolled back to their own display. A quick look reassured him that their display was at least as good as anyone else's — maybe better. "The junk-pile sellers won't have a chance!" he scoffed.

A moment later the doors opened and the first of the tourists wandered in. Since the Fruits of the Earth booth was well located, Tom had expected the tourists to come to their booth almost at once, but for some reason it didn't work that way. As if drawn by a magnet they all seemed to go straight for the junk piles. To Tom's disgust, he could hear them exclaiming over how cheap everything was, as they pawed through the piles of goods.

"How can they waste their time there when we've got such good stuff?" he demanded indignantly.

"Patience, my son," Andrew said with a grin. "He who sells last, sells most — at least that is what I fervently hope!"

At last a few tourists began examining other booths. One couple, toting two battered picture frames, came up to the Fruits of the Earth booth.

"Oh look," the lady exclaimed, pointing to a miniature garden Tom had planted in a large goldfish bowl. "It's just like a small rock garden! Are you boys looking after this booth for your father?"

"Heck no!" Tom said indignantly.

Andrew stood up and smiled in a friendly way.

"We're in business for ourselves, Ma'am," he said. "Everything we have on display in this section, including the miniature rock garden, is native to Canada — the plants to this region in particular. The rocks are largely from the northern part of the province."

"The rocks in this section" — his arm swept over the geodes — "are lava-formed minerals from the desert areas of Mexico and the southwestern United States. As you can see, they have been cut and polished to form ornamental bookends. The quartz here" — and he gestured to more of the rocks — "is all from Canada. It also makes unusual bookends or a coffee table conversation piece."

Andrew smiled again and Tom watched in awe as he deftly sold the lady and her husband a pair of the quartz bookends for twenty dollars.

"You amaze me," Tom said as the couple moved on. "I can see I'm going to be left with stock control, because I sure couldn't rhyme out a sales talk like that."

"It's not that hard," Andrew said self-consciously. "It just takes practice. I used to sell things at the science fair they have at school every year. By the end of the weekend you'll be doing the same thing easily."

Tom wasn't so sure, but he found that by noon he was handling customers with a fair bit of ease. He couldn't talk about what they had for sale as casually as Andrew did, but most of the people who stopped to browse or buy liked to hear about where the plants and rocks came from, and what it was like on the Escarpment. Tom found he was advising many of the tourists about where to find good secluded spots for picnics, or even telling them where they could locate an inexpensive restaurant in the area.

"Boy," he said to Andrew after trying to explain to yet another family of tourists where the nicest parks were within twenty miles, "I think for next week we should get some tourist information pamphlets."

Andrew grinned. "You are now fully initiated into the tourist industry," he said with mock solemnity. "Be glad to know that you are aiding in the prosperity of the area, the province, the country and the world."

Just then a bus load of senior citizens from Ohio arrived at the market, and Andrew and Tom were kept busy waiting on customers. When the rush finally subsided, Tom plopped into his chair in exhaustion.

"Boy," he said, "I never knew there were so many tourists!"

"It's the biggest industry in the world, and the second biggest in Canada," Andrew replied absently as he rearranged their depleted stock. The counter had begun to look very patchy.

By mid-afternoon the boys were wishing they had the things that had been ruined by the Cobras. Their sales had been good, and without the extra minerals and plants, their booth was beginning to look carelessly arranged and unattractive. Most of the tourists were just wandering by without bothering to stop and examine what they had for sale.

"I guess we should have had more stuff ready," Tom said wearily. The day had been more tiring than they had imagined it could be.

"Yeah," Andrew agreed slowly. "And you know what? We're going to have to spend all evening working like mad just to get enough stuff ready for tomorrow."

Tom groaned. He hadn't even thought about the next day.

At about five o'clock, Fruits of the Earth, Incorporated closed up shop for the night. There were only a few things left in the booth, so getting ready to go home didn't take long. The misery of knowing how much work they had to do that night was balanced only by the gleeful realization of how much they had sold that day.

Andrew carefully counted the cash they had taken in, while Tom sat on the edge of the booth gazing at the money in dreamy exhaustion.

"How much?" he demanded when Andrew had finished counting.

"One hundred and forty-eight dollars and fifty cents," he announced with relish.

"Wow!" Tom said. "I sure didn't think we'd do that well. At this rate we'll make our fortune in three weekends — maybe even two! Of course, though, we can't count on one customer buying three sets of bookends every day," he added with a grin. To the boys' great joy, one couple had spent almost sixty dollars at their booth just before noon.

"We still have things to pay for," Andrew reminded him. "But if the sales keep up we should do all right. First thing Monday morning we'll have to open a joint account at the bank."

"Yes," Tom said happily, "all that beautiful money should definitely be kept nice and safe in the bank."

For several minutes the two contemplated their riches. Then Mr. MacDonald arrived at the booth.

"Well, how did it go, boys?" he asked.

"Great!" Tom exclaimed.

"We did a lot better than we thought we would, Dad. In fact, we took in almost a hundred and fifty dollars!"

"You really did do all right," Mr. MacDonald said, looking noticeably impressed with their success. "I guess that means we don't have too much stuff to load into the car tonight."

It took only five minutes to load what was left. As they started for home, Tom and Andrew leaned back against the seats and tried not to think of the work they still had to do that night.

"By the way, boys," Mr. MacDonald said after a moment, "you won't be having any more trouble with the Cobras. The gang has been officially disbanded."

"Disbanded!" Tom repeated in amazement. "How come?"

"What did you do, Dad?" Andrew asked seriously. "We didn't want to cause any bad feelings if possible."

"The bad feelings were already there," his father pointed out. "I just went to the police and told them what happened."

"The police!" Tom hadn't realized before that when Mr. MacDonald had said the boys had broken the law, he had really meant it.

"That won't make things worse, will it, Dad?" Andrew asked anxiously. "They already had quite a grudge against Tom, and I hate to see it made worse."

"People can't go around wrecking private property just because they don't like you," Mr. MacDonald said. "And you can't let it go just because you think they really didn't mean it. But," he added, rubbing his hand over his chin, "I thought about that when I made the complaint. So I made the crux of my grievance the mess the Cobras made of my shed and the paint they wasted."

"What did the police do?" Tom asked apprehensively. Usually adults didn't see things the way kids did, and he was afraid of open warfare instead of the occasional hassling that had been going on before. He hated Billy, but he knew his enemy wasn't stupid. The president of the Cobras would blame Tom and Andrew for the trouble.

"The police were glad it had happened, actually," Mr. MacDonald said in amusement. "They'd noticed the gang and were afraid the boys might start out playing pranks and end up breaking into empty houses and that sort of thing. When I told them what had happened, they spent a few hours visiting the boys' parents. They recommended that the gang be disbanded and the parents were only too happy to agree. Mike Torsky's folks already called me to apologize and offered to pay for the damage."

"Can the guys still hang around together?" Tom asked suspiciously.

"Yes, the police can't stop that, although Mike has been forbidden to play with Billy," Mr. MacDonald said.

Tom leaned back in the seat again. The gang would still be there because the guys would still flock around Billy. Probably even Mike would be allowed to take part in things again after a week or two. But the Cobras might not be as vicious, he thought hopefully. Then he discarded the idea. Billy was spiteful, and as long as the guys were doing what he said, it would still be bad if there were no adults around.

The rest of the ride was completed in silence. When they reached the house they decided to leave the things in the car until the next day. Andrew walked Tom to the road.

"You know, Tom," he said, "if there are no more

Cobras, I guess there's no more initiation either. You won't be blackballed any longer, so your problem is solved. The guys will forget about thinking you're a chicken, especially if they want you on the football team they're going to start up towards the end of the summer to play other towns. So I was thinking — if you want, I could do a lot of the getting things ready and you could practise with them; I mean — if the sales got too much, you could pull out. There should be enough for your bicycle in another week or so . . . " Andrew's voice trailed off and his face turned red as he glanced shyly at Tom.

Tom looked at him in amazement. He knew Andrew well enough now to realize that he was saying Tom could go back with his old friends and forget about him, that there would be no hard feelings.

"I'm no good at sports," Andrew went on, "but I know you love them. So I don't want you to think you have to hang around here now if you don't want to." He had been staring at the ground during this speech, but when he finished he looked straight at Tom, his red face frowning slightly.

"You're nuts," Tom said, and smiled. He could feel a rising heat on his face too. "If there's time I might play ball with them for a bit, but what we're doing is too important. Besides," he added with a grin, "after being around a brain like you, I expect my friends to be at least a little bit intelligent, and those guys just don't qualify."

Andrew smiled self-consciously. "Well, okay," he said in obvious relief. "If you're sure."

"Yeah," Tom answered cheerfully as he pushed off on his bicycle, "I'm sure. I'll be back after supper and we'll get to work."

The cool evening air fanned the heat from Tom's face as he pedalled along the dusty road towards home. It wasn't entirely true, what he had said to Andrew. He would love to get back into sports, but he didn't think the initiation would be forgotten that easily.

Andrew didn't care that he was a chicken, but Andrew wasn't like the other guys. And besides, in the fall he would go back to his special school in Toronto and Tom would be odd man out again. Andrew knew what it was like to be the one nobody wanted to bother with; and so he'd offered Tom a way out.

Tom tried to force down the memory of the way he used to feel when he had been captain and all the guys had wanted to be on his team. They had crowded around him, eagerly paying attention to everything he had said. It had never occurred to him then how awful it could be to be alone all the time, to be the one who was always taken along grudgingly — or not at all. It had felt so good, being the one on top.

As the night sounds grew around him, Tom felt a bitter longing for the way things used to be.

10
Exploring

The days drifted by, punctuated by weekends of exhausting work for Tom and Andrew, selling the "fruits of the earth" they had made or gathered. Their bank account grew far more rapidly than either of them had anticipated. Their goods sold so fast that Tom had to spend at least two days a week making macramé plant hangers, while Andrew carefully cleaned rocks or chipped small pieces to be used in their Junior Geologist's Kits.

They had developed the kit one rainy afternoon after totalling up the number of small rock samples they sold to kids. Andrew had typed up a couple of pages with descriptions of various minerals and instructions designed for younger kids who wanted to start collecting. They had taken the sheets into St. Catharines and for eight dollars had had a hundred of each printed. The kits cost them less than a dollar each, but sold well for three.

At least one day a week they spent collecting and potting plants, and designing miniature gardens in goldfish bowls. Usually the two of them drifted up to the Escarpment on their free days anyway, just for the fun of exploring.

Tom began hiking down all the paths he could find, while Andrew chipped rocks and peered at stones, looking for fossils from the time when huge inland seas had covered the area. They found that fossils didn't sell to the tourists — only to the occasional rockhounds who stopped to chat at their booth. So the search was only for Andrew's own pleasure.

By mid-August, Tom felt they must know every inch of the Escarpment within thirty kilometres of their homes. At the end of July they had totalled their money and each had taken a third. Tom's share had been more than enough to buy the bicycle he had been dreaming of owning. Once he got it, he and Andrew ranged even farther along the Escarpment.

Today they had returned to the gorge. Of all the places they had explored, both secret and open, for some reason the gorge still seemed best.

Andrew wandered off to look for fossils and Tom began hiking in the opposite direction, downstream. Periodically he stopped to examine different plants, partly to see if they would be suitable for transplanting, but mostly because they now fascinated him.

He pulled a green pod off a milkweed plant and split it open. Inside, the immature seeds glistened white like the scales on the underside of a fish. Tom spread the tiny parachutes out on his fingers, feeling a cooling sensation as the filaments dried. He watched with a deep, nameless pleasure as the breeze caught them and carried them away, glinting in the sun. Vaguely he wondered if the Indians who used to roam the country-side had felt as peaceful as he did in the gorge.

Shaking off the reflective mood, he decided to search for a new way up the cliff on the opposite side of the waterfall. Near the top there were huge chunks of rock, almost hidden by the bushes. From there, if he could reach them, Tom guessed he would be able to see almost everything that went on in the basin of the waterfall, and probably be close enough to feel the spray as well, if the wind was in the right direction.

Once the decision was made, Tom ran most of the way to the waterfall. By the time he reached it he was so out of breath that he collapsed onto a soft patch of grass by the stream to recoup his strength.

A moment later Andrew joined him, flopping down onto the soft growth, his legs sprawling awkwardly in the grass.

"Find anything?" Tom inquired casually.

"Nothing unusual," Andrew replied, squinting his eyes up against the sun. "Isn't it about time for some lunch? I'm starved with all this rock-pile stuff."

Without any further talk they dug into the knapsack and began devouring their lunches.

"I'm going to try and find a path up the side of the gorge over there by that rock," Tom said when they had finished.

Andrew looked appraisingly at the cliff where Tom was pointing. "Might be some good fossils up there," he commented. "If you find a path you think my limbs might manage, I'd like to inspect some of those shelves and outcroppings part way up."

"You know," Tom said teasingly, "if someone offered to take you on a climb up Mount Everest, you'd probably go — you'd figure you'd find some interesting mineral formations under the snow."

Andrew grinned, but didn't offer any argument. Instead he lay back in the grass with his hands behind his head. "I'll just lie here and let you be the explorer and do the work," he said.

Tom threw a handful of grass in his face, then stood up and stared at the cliff side, searching for a place where he could climb up. First of all he had to cross the stream, though. He didn't mind wading, of course, but it occurred to him that maybe there was a way behind the waterfall itself.

He sauntered over towards the falls, trying to ignore the silent, gaping mouth of the Black Tunnel a little up the gorge to his left. Each time they came into the gorge Tom tried to ignore the Tunnel, tried to pretend he didn't care about it any more. He never thought of the Cobra's initiation or the lost jack-knife now. He thought only of the Tunnel, waiting disdainfully for him to prove to himself that he wasn't a chicken after all.

Maybe he should try again now, Tom thought. Immediately he felt a lump forming in his throat and his stomach beginning to churn.

"Maybe later," he muttered to himself. He ran towards the waterfall, but even with the exciting feel of the spray on his face, he felt guilty about the Tunnel.

I just say later so I won't feel bad about not doing it now, he thought. But it's me I'm trying to fool, and it never works — so I feel rotten anyway. Damn that Billy and his damned initiation!

Tom's fists clenched. But he knew the fault was in himself. Billy had just found the weakness — he hadn't made it.

"I *will* do it," Tom said fiercely, glaring at the Tunnel. "I'll find this path and then I'll do it."

This time he meant it. He really meant it. But first he would find a way behind the waterfall and up the gorge.

Normally Tom wouldn't have found the path behind the falls because he would have been too cautious to risk climbing over the loose, slippery rocks flanking the curtain of water. As the cold water tumbled over the rocks, the spray dripped down his face and off the end of his nose. Forgetting all about the Tunnel, Tom laughed from the tickling feel of it.

Then carefully he began to edge his way behind the water. There was a ledge! Not a big one, but wide enough to walk on.

For a long time Tom stood behind the falls, listening to the roar of the water, feeling the cold spray, relishing the feeling of being hidden away from everything and everyone. The roar of the waterfall, the smell of the dampness and the cold of the spray filled his senses, and the hypnotic dancing of light through the streaming water held him motionless.

Suddenly he was aware that Andrew was beside him, frantically gripping the slippery, moss-covered rocks.

"You okay, Tom?" he shouted above the roar of the water. A look of relief was spreading over his bony face.

"Of course," Tom shouted back. He put out a hand to steady his friend, then together they moved along the path to the other side of the falls.

"What were you doing in there?" Tom demanded. "Those rocks are really slippery. With your sense of balance, you're lucky you didn't kill yourself. I would have helped you if I'd known you were coming."

Andrew blushed slightly. "I thought maybe something had happened to you," he explained with embarrassment. "I saw you sort of slipping and sliding over the stones, and then you went behind the falls. I waited and waited for you to come out. I called, but you didn't answer," he went on earnestly, "so I figured I had better make sure you hadn't slipped and fallen."

Tom looked at him in amazement. "You're absolutely and completely nuts," he stated firmly. "If it had been bad enough for me to fall, chances are you would have ended up doing involuntary cartwheels."

"Well, I couldn't just sit there," Andrew said. "I thought we were going exploring anyway."

Tom laughed and pretended to punch Andrew. They had a vigorous boxing match, never really hitting each other, until finally Andrew's legs somehow tangled and he went down.

Both laughing, they began searching for a way up the cliff. While Tom tried climbing where it looked possible, Andrew peered up the side, trying to see what kinds of rocks lay between the trees and the bushes that grew in irregular patches.

"How about over there," he called, pointing to a spot near the waterfall where some of the rock had broken away to expose a clean face of limestone and shale.

Tom looked up. "I don't think we can do it," he called. "The rock looks too loose. We'd probably slide on our backsides all the way down and into the rocky part of the stream."

"I think that action should be avoided at all costs," Andrew remarked mock-seriously.

"Yeah, I think so too," Tom agreed. "But we should be able to get to that chunk of rock up there," he added, pointing to the area where the rock he had chosen as a lookout reared out of the ground.

Andrew studied the place where Tom pointed. "It might be all right up there for specimens," he finally agreed. "I haven't had much luck so far down by the stream, so we may as well try there."

The climb was slower than Tom would have liked, because Andrew had none of his agility for scrambling and climbing. When the pace became unbearably tedious, Tom would branch off sideways looking for other ways to climb, or for secret places where they could rest, hidden from the world.

In the back of his mind he had a practical purpose for his search. The last time they had been to the gorge, he had found a couple of burnt-out campfires and a grotesquely angular cobra scratched onto a rock. With a sense of shock Tom had realized that Billy and the others had invaded the gorge. He had a grim feeling in the pit of his stomach that he and Andrew would be wise to avoid them now, especially in a place as secluded as the gorge. Billy would blame them for setting the police on the Cobras, regardless of what the adults thought. Yes, he had to find a few places where he and Andrew could disappear if the Cobras showed up in a nasty mood.

Tom guessed that the impetus for the Cobras was dying out because of the police intervention, but he had seen the sullen glare in Billy's eyes. Billy hated Tom even more now, and the chorus of "Chicken Man" had become vicious rather than idle. If the guys were all there with him, he might start a real fight down in the gorge where there were no adults to stop it. Tom hated to think what could happen then. He shivered a little as if a cold breeze had slipped over his bare arms. He and Andrew should definitely find a few private places where the others would never find them.

Andrew scrambled up beside him on a fern-edged ledge halfway up the slope. "I'm exhausted," he muttered and lay panting on his back.

Tom grinned at him and continued to look out from behind the screen of ferns into the gorge.

"I noticed that our friends have also been enjoying the scenic pleasures of the gorge," Andrew said casually after a minute or so.

"Yeah, and I'm not too keen on meeting up with them down there. If we do see them, we can disappear behind the waterfall or maybe come up here."

"Wouldn't hurt. I don't think they're too fond of either of us right now, and I have no wish to engage in hand to hand combat. We'd lose for sure."

Tom laughed and stood up. "I'm going to climb up there to that rock," he said, pointing to his lookout. "Coming?"

"Nope," Andrew replied lazily. "I've had enough of risking my neck for one day."

"If I see anything that looks like a fossil, I'll bring it

back," Tom said as he started climbing up the slope.

It felt good to pit his muscles against the slope and the rock. He liked the smell of the bushes and of the tufts of grass he used as handholds. His hands and knees stung from the scraping and pulling, but it felt good. It felt very good.

Finally he reached the earth-covered ledge where the rock lay. Behind it was a bare, jagged wall. Tom looked closely for a minute and saw some markings he thought might be fossils. But since he didn't really know, he abandoned his half-hearted search and climbed up onto the rock.

"Hello down there!" he shouted to Andrew. He could hear Andrew's laugh floating up on the breeze as he waved. Tom lay down on the rock and gazed out over the gorge. The view was terrific, better than he had thought it would be.

He could see everything around the waterfall's basin, right back to the gaping hole of the first tunnel half-way up the cliff. From that point he got only glimpses of things along the gorge, unless they were right beside or actually in the stream. Past the second waterfall, the stream curved and nothing but the deep green sway of trees could be seen.

Tom noticed another path snaking its way up the side of the gorge almost to where he lay. It looked like a much-used rabbit path — worn on the ground but with bits of bushes overhanging it. He sat up to see it more clearly and decided to try it on the way down. It might be an easier way for Andrew to climb up to the rock. He could see that his friend had already scrambled down the bank and was poking among the rocks that lined the stream.

Carefully Tom edged himself to the top of the path. It was steep, but not a sheer drop With one hand gripping the slim, tough branches of a willow bush, he began slipping down. He tried to grip with his feet, while he looked for another handhold.

The path was muddy from the almost nightly showers of rain, but there were small rocks and roots sticking out of the ground to wedge his feet on. The middle section was easy, but the last two metres were straight up and down, dropping directly onto the bank of the stream. Tom didn't mind jumping, but he didn't see how Andrew would be able to manage. His feet would shoot out as though he'd landed on banana peels instead of the loose shale.

While Tom sat on the edge of the drop swinging his legs and pondering the situation, Andrew strolled over and looked up at him.

"Playing Humpty Dumpty?" he asked with a grin.

"That's gratitude," Tom said in mock annoyance. "I try to find a rabbit path exclusively for you, and all I get is sarcasm!"

Andrew eyed the two-metre drop. "It's amazing how high rabbits can jump these days," he remarked dryly.

Tom looked at him, looked at the drop and then scrambled to his feet. Quickly he back-tracked a short distance and examined the path.

"Boy, am I dumb!"

The path had taken a sharp left-hand turn under some low bushes and emerged again along a narrow ledge which widened into a gentle slope leading to the gravel surrounding the stream.

"Well, here's our secret route up to the lookout rock," Tom yelled as he bounded the rest of the way down the path.

Andrew was examining the rock face at the drop. "Great," he called absent-mindedly. He started chipping at a loose piece of the rock, and it appeared to be absorbing all his attention. Tom watched for a moment, hesitating. Should he go up and through the Black Tunnel now, while no one was noticing? He would do it this time for sure. After all, he couldn't spend the rest of his life being afraid of something as ordinary as the dark. Still, he was reluctant to let even Andrew know he was going to try it.

But as he looked up towards the gaping mouth of the Tunnel, his sense of the ordinary world began to waver. The sounds of the falling water and the steady *chip, chip* of Andrew's hammer began to sound all out of proportion. And his feet and legs felt cold and half-numbed as he sloshed, head down, through the stream towards the black hole.

But this time he would do it.

11
One last try

Tom's feet still felt too heavy as he walked over the broken shale and bits of rock on the bank of the stream. His palms were wet and slippery as he scrambled up the short gravel slope leading to the Tunnel.

"It'll be a snap," he muttered hoarsely to himself. "They'll see. There's nothing chicken about me."

Suddenly his feet slipped on the gravel and he fell to his hands and knees. Wiping a bit of oozing blood off his hands onto his jeans, he looked up towards the waiting Tunnel. Silent . . . black . . . so very cold.

He swallowed and started back up the slope, forcing himself to be more careful. His gripping fear retreated a little.

After what seemed like a long time, Tom once again stood at the mouth of the Tunnel. In the background he could hear Andrew's hammer and the gentle rustle of leaves. And he could hear the slow, even *drip, drip* as the seeping water sweated through the cold rock and fell into the still pools covering the Tunnel floor. He felt the warm sunshine on his back and the dank coolness of the breeze issuing from the Tunnel on his cheek.

"I'm not afraid," he said defiantly. His voice sounded odd. Tom could hear a tortured echo of it bounce back from the black bowels of the Tunnel.

Carefully he sloshed forward. The muddy water seeped through his shoes and turned his pant legs stiff and heavy at the bottom. Without stopping, he walked to the niche where he had waited out the storm. A few steps farther and he would be past the rusted pins that had once held the grille.

Tom stopped. All summer he had been practising moving around his room, and finally the whole house, with all the lights turned off. He could do that. Now he could do this.

"Just you wait," he said fiercely, trying to hurl his thoughts against the drooling throat of the Black Tunnel. "I'm not scared any more. I'm not scared of anything. Nothing!"

Again the eerie echoes drifted back to his ears.

And everywhere else in the Tunnel was silence. A terrible, deep silence.

Drip, drip.

The drops splashed into the pools around Tom's feet. The cold breath of the Tunnel swished around his arms and face. The silence continued — indifferent, hungry, waiting silence.

Tom heard his heart thumping. He swallowed and desperately forced his feet to shuffle a little farther into the black sliminess. "I'm not scared!" he shouted hoarsely. And the echoes swirled back mockingly.

He stumbled to the throat of the Tunnel, barely noticing the rusty grille in the water-covered muck beneath his feet. "You see, I'm not scared at all!" he shouted desperately. He felt the cold darkness getting closer. "I'm no chicken! You can tell Billy. You can tell everybody. I'm no chicken!"

The echoes swished back again, mingling eerily with the slow, even drip.

Tom forced his legs past the throat. This was the Tunnel itself. He could feel the darkness closing in. He could hardly breathe. There was the darkness, the giant squeezing at his chest. Tom's mind heaved with fear. Desperately, clinging wildly to the idea that he had to go on, Tom put out a hand to steady himself. His fingers touched the rock. Years of slime and wetness curled into his hand.

He screamed. His legs buckled and he fell into the water. He felt the cold splashing over his face. He tasted the raw taste of slimy rock. Desperately, crawling and scrambling, Tom staggered back to the throat, into the mouth of the Tunnel.

And then the sunlight! He felt the warm sunlight on his face. He began sobbing wildly.

He fell, and Andrew was beside him. For a moment Andrew put his arms around him, holding him the way his father had done, safe from a nightmare.

Then Tom's mind cleared a little. "Get away from me!" he shouted. Viciously he pushed his friend away and scrambled to his feet.

Andrew fell, sprawling. "Tom!" he shouted urgently, shock surging over his face.

"Go to hell!"

Tom ran. He ran down along the stream, tripping over roots and plants. He knew he was crying but he didn't care. Frantically he scrambled up the cliff and found his bicycle. He felt as though his body wouldn't go any farther, but if he stayed there Andrew would find him. He couldn't talk to anyone now. No one.

He pushed his bicycle to the other side of the field and slid it into the gully where he had found his other one wrecked. Then he slid down into the green grass, hidden from the world. For a long time he cried into the grass. Then the wretchedness became too much; a kind of numbing resignation slipped over him and he fell asleep.

When he woke up Tom still felt quietly resigned, and he almost hoped he would continue to feel so emotionless. But already he could feel the nagging shame starting at the back of his mind.

He had failed again.

But no, it wasn't failure any longer. It was complete

nothingness. He knew now that he would never be like other people; he would never be the kind of person he wanted to be.

For a moment he thought of running away, but miserably he decided he wouldn't be able to manage even that successfully. Besides, there would always be another Billy. It didn't matter. There was something wrong with him. Tom felt a terrible sinking dread as he thought of going crazy. Not just pretend, but really crazy. There would be doctors and strange smells and worried looks. And there would always be the terrible feeling that there was something wrong with him. That he was different. That he was alone.

Well, he might as well get used to it. He would really be alone now. He felt sick as he thought of how he had hit his friend. But Andrew had seen him run, had heard him cry. He wouldn't come back now. There would be no whispers or jeers, because Andrew wasn't like that. But he wouldn't come back.

Wearily Tom pushed his bicycle along the lane and onto the road. He didn't have much energy to get on and ride, but finally he did.

The cool wind felt good. Tom began to return to normal. Vaguely he wondered if his mind was like a jigsaw puzzle with one of the pieces lost. That was the way he felt.

But he still didn't feel crazy. He wondered if someone would feel crazy if he were insane, and decided he would. A person might be too scared and hurt to think about whether his mind was right, but if he ever had a chance to think, a calm period when he felt safe again, then he'd have to know.

At the bottom of the hill, Tom hesitated. Maybe if he went over to Andrew's and said he was sorry . . . But then the shocked look on his friend's face flashed bitterly in Tom's memory. And Andrew must have watched him screaming and crawling too.

A drowning shame swept over Tom, and then it changed to anger. Andrew had spied on him! He wasn't going to say he was sorry to that jerk. It was none of his business anyway.

He pushed off again and pedalled furiously towards home. For sure Andrew would think he was crazy now, and Tom would be unable to explain. Well, he didn't care if he never saw Andrew again!

It was almost dark by the time Tom reached home. He didn't see Andrew sitting in the ditch between the road and the hedge until he was right alongside him.

"Tom!" Andrew said suddenly, scrambling to his feet.

Tom wanted desperately to talk to him, to tell him he was sorry and hadn't meant to hit out at him. But instead all he said was, "What are you doing here?"

Andrew looked surprised and a little hurt. "I wanted to make sure you were okay, that's all."

"Well, I am." Tom was going to say more, but all of a sudden Andrew stood up straight.

"Sorry to butt in," he said fiercely, and Tom realized with a shock that he was really angry. Somehow he had never imagined that Andrew could get so angry.

"Guess I'll be going then," Andrew added, with a hard edge to his voice.

"Well, go then," Tom spat out. He couldn't cope with this. His feelings and the memories of the day became mixed up in his mind and he couldn't think straight.

But he watched in dismay as Andrew left. Now he had really done it. Andrew would never come back now. Not after today. And the worst of it was that Tom knew everything was his fault.

Wretchedly he put his bicycle away and went into the house. "Well, it's about time you condescended to come home," his mother said angrily when he went into the kitchen. He looked at her in surprise. Of course she would be angry. It was more than two hours past dinner time.

"I won't have you inconveniencing and worrying your mother like this," his father added sternly. "It doesn't matter how good a time you are having with Andrew. You can have the courtesy to come in on time for dinner."

It isn't fair, Tom thought.

"Just stop picking on me!" he shouted at them. He slammed the kitchen door behind him and ran up to his bedroom.

"Tom!"

"Go to hell!" Tom screamed down the stairs.

Then he pulled off his clothes and got into bed. He was trembling and he felt cold all over. Fearfully he wondered what his parents were going to do now. He was too old to be spanked and they hadn't really punished him in a long time. He would never be able to explain what had happened today. And they wouldn't understand that he hadn't really meant it when he swore at them. He should go apologize. But he was sure if he moved he would start to cry again. Then he would have to explain, and he just couldn't.

But he had to say he was sorry. If his parents were angry there wouldn't be anybody left who would have anything to do with him. Tom forced himself to get out of bed. His stomach felt sick from all the emotions churning through him. But he had to go apologize. He hadn't really meant it anyway.

As he went out the door, his parents were coming along the hall towards his room. They both looked grim and worried and angry all at once.

"Look," Tom said quickly, before they could say anything. He felt he couldn't bear it if they said how shocked and hurt they were. "I'm sorry. I didn't mean to yell at you like that. I — I had a fight with Andrew, and I don't feel very well either."

Suddenly he knew he really didn't feel well. Desperately he ran to the bathroom. He was just in time.

It wasn't very pleasant being sick to his stomach from

his ragged emotions, but it made his parents forget about being angry with him. His mother put him to bed and brought him a bowl of home-made soup for his supper.

"You must have the flu," she said in concern. "That's why you acted so unlike yourself. I don't want you getting out of bed tomorrow until I say it's all right. Don't forget. Now have a good sleep."

She turned out the light and left his room. Tom knew it wasn't the flu, but he didn't have the energy to argue. He didn't really care whether he got up tomorrow or not anyway. Even if he did get up, there was nothing to do.

Wearily he turned over onto his stomach. He thought he would probably lie awake all night, but he was too tired. In a few seconds he had fallen fast asleep.

12
Keep away
from those tunnels!

The next two days were just as miserable as Tom had expected them to be. His mother still thought he had the flu because of the way he moped around, and since it poured rain both days, she wasn't about to let him go outside.

Tom had an urge to go off by himself to try and straighten out his thoughts, to decide what to do. The need to get away was so strong that he argued with his mother almost constantly on the second day. By the time his father came home from work, he was thoroughly in disgrace again.

Dinner was a silent, strained meal. It was with a feeling of relief that Tom offered to do the dishes. At least he could be alone, and his mother would stop being mad at him. Right then he hated himself so much that his mother's displeasure was more than he could handle.

Dully, he wondered how Andrew was doing, whether or not he was still angry. The next day was Friday and they didn't have anything ready for their booth. With a sinking feeling it occurred to him that probably Andrew didn't want him to help with it any more.

As he put away the last dish, Tom noticed that the rain had finally stopped. With a strange sense of deliverance he slipped out the kitchen door and into the cool freshness of the evening. For awhile he walked aimlessly down the road towards town. Then he paused and sat down on the wet rocks of an ornamental stone fence surrounding a vacant lot.

For a long while Tom just sat and thought about everything that had happened. There was no doubt about it now. He really was a chicken, at least about dark, closed-in places. And probably he would never get over it either. Always, always he would be different and alone.

"Wonder why it had to happen to me?" he muttered glumly to himself. But there wasn't much point in dwelling on it — it had happened and he had to live with it.

"But why should it be such a big thing to everybody?" he argued with himself. Nobody cared that Billy was a coward and a crybaby and a bully. That was a lot worse. So why should everybody make such a big thing of his being scared of being closed up in a dark place?

Tom was still brooding over the unfairness of things when he heard tires crunching over the gravel of the road. It was Andrew.

"Hey, Andrew," Tom called without thinking. Too

late he remembered that Andrew probably wasn't talking to him any more. He stood up and bit his lower lip, expecting to be snubbed.

Instead Andrew stopped his bike and looked at Tom a little uncertainly.

"Hi," he said finally, in a quiet voice.

"Where you going?" Tom asked, trying to sound natural and wondering desperately how to apologize for what he had done.

"I was coming to see you," Andrew replied. He tugged at his hair the way he always did when he was unsure of himself. "We have to plan what we're going to sell this weekend. I mean we have to get the stuff ready."

"Yeah," Tom said shortly. There was a strained silence as each of the boys tried to think what to say next. Both of them stared at the ground self-consciously.

"Andrew," Tom said suddenly, "I — I'm sorry I yelled at you and knocked you down and everything. I mean — well — I'm sorry, that's all."

He looked up defiantly, waiting for Andrew to yell at him and tell him off.

But the other boy just blushed slightly. "Yeah, okay," he said shyly. "I guess I didn't act too smart either. I should have known you wanted to be by yourself. Anyway, let's forget it."

"Okay," Tom said in relief.

Silently they walked along the road towards Tom's house. But even though Andrew had said to forget the whole thing, Tom was afraid his friend must secretly think he was crazy. "You know," he said finally, speaking quickly, "I thought about everything a lot. I mean — I'm sure I'm not crazy or anything."

Andrew looked at him in surprise. "Were you thinking you were? No wonder you were so overwrought."

Tom wasn't quite sure what he meant, but he could tell Andrew didn't think he was crazy. "I just figure I'm scared of dark, closed-in places," he went on more confidently, hoping he was explaining how he felt.

"Yes," Andrew said in obvious bewilderment, looking at Tom. "A lot of people are afraid of that — or of something else."

"Yeah," Tom agreed glumly, "but other people aren't as chicken as I am — or at least it doesn't show."

"Most people," Andrew said, "avoid the things they are terrified of. They do it quietly so no one notices. They don't keep ramming themselves into it and then think they're off balance simply because they respond with fear to what they knew they were afraid of in the first place. You just had the bad luck to have your pet fear paraded for everyone to see."

"Yeah, I sure did."

"You know," Andrew went on earnestly, "you really shouldn't keep forcing yourself to go into that tunnel.

It's like trying to cure a fear of guns by playing Russian roulette every night. I don't see how it will do any good and it could do a lot of harm."

"I don't know what you're talking about," Tom said guardedly.

"What I mean," the other said thoughtfully, "is that you've picked the biggest thing you could find to try and cure yourself. Heck, I'm nervous about going into that tunnel and I've never been afraid of things like that. Why don't you just start small — I don't know — leave the lights off when you go to the bathroom at night, that kind of thing."

He peered hopefully at Tom, wondering if he would accept his advice.

"Yeah, maybe," was all Tom said. How could he tell Andrew that he'd been doing that all summer and so far it had only helped a little bit? At this rate, he thought dismally, it would take him years to get over being afraid.

But at least one good thing had happened. He and Andrew were still friends even though Andrew had seen him at his absolute worst.

They spent the rest of the evening making plans for the weekend sale. By the time Andrew left, the old footing had been re-established. Cheerfully they made plans to spend all day Friday getting their goods ready.

Saturday morning Tom and Andrew set up their booth in record time. By now they knew all the regular people at the other booths; so they spent a few minutes wandering around getting the news and admiring the new crafts and other things on display.

"I don't think we're going to get much business today," one girl told Tom.

"How come?" he asked in surprise.

"The weather report says it's going to start raining around mid-morning."

"Think it will last all day?" They had made a good overall profit so far, but Tom hated not making enough money to cover their expenses for the day — and they might not, if the weather was bad.

"It's supposed to rain non-stop until tonight," the girl replied. "Tomorrow too, according to the radio. At least it will give me a chance to catch up on all my orders from the people around here."

She set up a small hand loom and began working at stringing it up for her weaving. She waved goodbye when Tom wandered off.

Andrew was standing by the door looking gloomily at the cloud-covered sky. Tom walked over and stood beside him. The clouds were steel grey. Over the lake they were purple-black.

"Looks as if we're really in for it again," Tom said gloomily. "If it rains as hard as those clouds say it will, we won't do much business."

"It's hard to tell," Andrew replied. "Who knows? Maybe people will stop to get out of the rain."

"Maybe," Tom said without too much hope.

In fact it was the worst day they had had since the start of the summer. The only thing they sold was one three-dollar Junior Geologist Kit. The rain poured down in sheets without any letup. The irritating drumming of the raindrops on the roof above their heads didn't stop all day, although once in awhile it was drowned out by peals of thunder.

When Tom's father came to pick them up late in the afternoon, he was worried about the water. The fields were flooding because the rain had come down so hard and fast it hadn't had a chance to soak into the ground. The car splashed through pool after pool of water that covered the road. Tom and Andrew stared dismally at the familiar landscape that now looked so different.

"Boy, now I know how Noah felt," Andrew said as he stepped out of the car into the puddle that surrounded his house.

The next day, however, the rain slowed to a dull drizzle, and business at the flea market was a bit better. Still Tom and Andrew quickly saw that they would just break even, despite the whole weekend's work.

"I didn't know going into business could be so frustrating," Tom complained after he had failed to make a sale for the fifth time in a row.

"It might get better," Andrew answered. "The sky seems to be clearing, so maybe we'll get more customers."

About midway in the afternoon, Tom saw Mr. Piers threading his way through the tourists towards their booth.

"Hello, boys. How's business?" he inquired cheerfully.

"Not very good," Andrew answered.

"Can we sell you anything?" Tom asked with a grin.

"No, no thanks. I just stopped by to tell you boys to watch out for the tunnels tomorrow if you're down in the gorge. I have to go away for the day, so I won't be there to make sure you don't get caught in it."

"In what, sir?" Andrew asked in bewilderment.

"In the runoff, of course," Mr. Piers went on. "With all this rain, they've decided to let some of the water run out of the reservoir before the pressure gets too high and they have problems. Tomorrow at two o'clock they're going to send all the surplus water through the tunnels. If you got caught in that, besides being drowned, you'd be so bashed up against the tunnel walls and the rocks in the stream that your own mother wouldn't recognize you when she came to identify the body. So keep away from those tunnels tomorrow."

Mr. Piers shook his finger emphatically.

"For sure," Tom agreed. "Is it safe to be in the gorge?"

"Oh yes," Mr. Piers said. "The water will go right into the stream and the banks are high enough to keep it there. You'd only be in trouble if you were caught right in the tunnel. They'll let just a little out first so as long as you were outside you'd have time to get out of the way. But stay out of the tunnels altogether, just to be safe."

"Not much chance of *me* being in the Tunnel," Tom muttered bitterly.

"Don't like it in there, eh?" Mr. Piers said sympathetically. "It's too messy and wet for my tastes too. Well, I had better get going. I just wanted to stop by and let you know about it. You're about the only kids who know how to get down there, so I guess that's good enough. Be seeing you, boys."

"So long," they called.

"We'll have to keep our things out of the way of the water," Andrew remarked casually.

A couple of tourists wandered over to the booth then, and both Tom and Andrew forgot about the Tunnel in their efforts to sell a souvenir.

"Everything we have displayed is of Canadian origin," Tom said as the man and his wife casually examined their goods.

"With the exception of the geodes," Andrew mentioned conscientiously. "They're lava rock formations from Mexico."

"But they were cleaned and cut here in Canada," Tom added quickly. He looked sternly at Andrew, who started to laugh.

"They would make an unusual souvenir for our

neighbours," the lady said.

"Whatever you think, honey," her husband remarked in obvious boredom.

"Well, they're very nice," the lady said again, uncertainly.

As always, Tom was tempted to order her to make up her mind, but he'd learned from Andrew that this was the time when a carefully chosen word from the salesman might tip the balance. He bit his lip and tried to decide what would convince her the best.

"Most of the people who buy our minerals say they like them because they are absolutely unique," he said cautiously, looking for a change in the woman's expression that would show him he was on the right track. Nothing.

"And of course, because our expenses are low and my partner does all the buying and finishing himself," Tom went on quickly, "we are able to sell high quality ornaments at about half of what anyone else sells them for."

"They do seem reasonable," the lady said hesitantly.

Andrew carefully picked up one of the rocks that was covered with irregular teeth of purple crystals. Even though he was interested in selling the mineral, he handled it lovingly, Tom noticed.

"Perhaps you'd rather have a coffee table ornament, instead of bookends," he said with a smile. "This rock isn't as flashy as some of them, but just look at these crystals." He held the rock out for the lady's inspection.

"What are they?" she asked dubiously.

"Amethysts in their natural state," Andrew said simply. "Jewellers charge a lot of money for cut stones like these, but actually, north of Lake Superior amethysts like these are fairly common."

"Are they flawed?" the woman asked with more interest.

"No, ma'am," Andrew said with a smile, knowing now that she was sold. "They're good quality. Large ones, too," he added, pointing gently to a couple of crystals that were almost as large as his fingernail. "You can't find a more natural and at the same time a more impressive souvenir than semi-precious stones lying in their natural state. They're very subtle and very beautiful," he finished softly.

"Well, I guess we'll take that then," she said eagerly.

Tom made change while Andrew carefully wrapped the rock in tissue paper. When the couple had gone, Tom leaned back in his chair and looked at the goods they had on display.

"Funny thing," he said finally. "You always seem to sell the rocks but I always seem to sell the plants and macramé plant holders. I wonder why?"

Andrew flopped into his chair and tried to put his feet up on the counter, slipped, then settled into a more upright posture.

"Well," he said, "it's fairly obvious. You really think plants are special and I think rocks are special. I guess we're so enthusiastic about them that the customers look at them in a different way." He paused for a minute and his eyes narrowed slightly.

"Looks as if some of our friends decided to drop by," he said in a hardened voice.

Tom looked down the aisle. Billy, Skinner, and a couple of other former Cobras were sauntering towards them. He could feel the muscles in his stomach tense. He had a terrible fear that they might somehow know he had made a fool of himself at the Tunnel again. Stupid. They couldn't know.

Billy stopped in front of the counter with his hands stuck aggressively on his hips. Skinner and the other two leaned against the counter and began to finger the objects for sale with obvious disdain.

"Well," Billy said in exaggerated surprise, "Chicken Man and the String-Bean Brain. Isn't this cosy? Your own dumb little business. How much have you lost so far?"

The other three boys snickered.

"Hey, Chicken Man," Skinner said in a high nasal voice, "how much are you charging for this garbage?" He pushed a hanging planter so that it swayed dangerously in the air.

"If you want to buy something," Andrew said coldly,

"we'd be glad to sell it to you. Otherwise we would appreciate it if you would go away."

"Is that friendly?" Billy asked with sneering affability. "You know the Cobras don't like goofs like you who talk big."

"The Cobras have been disbanded," Tom said, looking straight at Billy.

Billy stared back and then a smile turned up the corners of his mouth. But his eyes became as cold and hard as pebbles. "You're all wrong, Chicken Man," he said softly. "The Cobras have been lying low, but that's all over with now. I've decided we should become active again. After all, we've got important things to do."

"Yeah, sure," Tom sneered. "Big shots like you — maybe you have to make sure your diapers get changed. That's about all I can think of."

"Listen to the Chicken Man!" Skinner taunted. Billy stood stock still while the other two fidgeted nervously.

"We had a council of war this morning, Chicken Man," Billy said slowly. He turned and began walking away. Casually he looked over his shoulder at Tom and Andrew. "You see," he said grimly, "we're going to get you, Chicken Man. We're going to get you good."

13
The perfect specimen

"Wow!" Andrew said as the Cobras walked away. "I had no idea Billy could be so vicious. I think the other two guys looked a little worried, though. What do you think?"

"I think Billy's really serious," Tom said vaguely. Everything seemed unreal. "I don't see why he hates me so much. I mean, I can't stand him either, but jeez, I wouldn't work that hard at getting even with him. Besides, I haven't done anything for him to get even with me for."

"I don't think Billy needs a reason," Andrew said grimly. "His intelligence is not of the highest order, and his personality is hardly the stuff of which saints are made. He hates you, Tom, because he can't push you around. You manage to show him up when he's at his worst." Andrew looked at his friend. "You probably don't even know you're doing it."

"He's weird, all right," Tom said, regretting that he

couldn't string words together the way Andrew could when he was angry.

While they packed up for the afternoon, Tom tried to figure out why Billy hated him so. There was no doubt he blamed Tom for the trouble with the police, and naturally he hadn't liked it when Tom had beat him up. But that couldn't be the real reason.

Then he began to remember little things that had happened when Tom was still the leader and Billy was the new kid. He had let Billy come along with the crowd even though he had kept trying to upset things and to get everyone picking on one person   usually Skinner. Finally Tom had put a stop to it. Once he had even told Billy in front of everyone that if he wanted things that way he wasn't welcome.

With a sick feeling of contempt, Tom remembered the way Billy had made up to him afterwards, treating him like his best friend. He had never noticed things like that very much then, but now he realized that that was when Billy's face had become hard and sullen — when he was being the nicest to Tom. The thought of it made him feel sick to his stomach. How could he have been so stupid, not to realize what kind of person Billy really was?

But then Tom understood — when he had been leader it didn't matter to him that Billy was a bully. He had assumed Billy could do no harm and so he had tolerated him so long as he kept in line. And until the time was right, Billy had kept in line.

"You know," Tom said finally to Andrew as they waited in the parking lot for Mr. MacDonald. "Billy acted like my best friend until he found out what a chicken I was."

The feeling and the words still hurt. Would they always hurt? Could people who hurt as he did carry it their whole lives and never be able to empty it away? Suddenly Tom saw his whole life stretching ahead, full of doing everything people thought he should do, but never really being free of the heavy feeling inside. Tom rubbed his head, feeling as though everything was all tilted around inside him.

"I hate Billy," he said suddenly, violently. "I'd sure like to get back at him."

Andrew looked at him in surprise.

"Wouldn't you like to get back at him?" Tom demanded.

Andrew shrugged. "My dad's here," he pointed out, without answering.

On the drive home Tom thought of different ways to get even with Billy. Without thinking about what he was doing, he agreed to meet Andrew the next morning at the pharmacy and spend the rest of the day in the gorge.

By the time he sat down to dinner he had devised about ten different ways to show Billy up for what he really was. There was a grim satisfaction in that, but eventually Tom realized that he felt more depressed than ever. When he'd finished helping his mother with the dishes, he wandered outside.

"Damn Billy," he hissed through clenched teeth. It didn't make him feel any better.

In a wave of misery Tom realized that what was wrong was himself. He was a chicken. There was no way around it, and he didn't feel like trying to beat it any more.

"Well, I guess that's it," he said softly to the trees. "I'll just have to learn to live with it."

The funny thing was, even resignation didn't help him feel any better. If he fought it he just made a fool of himself. But when he gave in he felt rotten anyway. There just didn't seem to be any sense to anything.

Tom still didn't feel much better the next morning as he waited for Andrew on the pharmacy steps. It was a gorgeous day, all sunshine and warmth, with just the right touch of a breeze. But these things didn't offset the rotten feeling in the pit of his stomach.

Finally Andrew came out.

"What took you so long?" Tom asked with an edge to his voice.

Andrew looked at him in surprise. "Sorry," he said after a minute. "I had to help Dad stock the shelves."

"Okay," Tom said, feeling ashamed of himself and even more bad tempered as a result. Everything seemed to irritate him this morning. If he didn't get off on his own for a bit, he was sure to start a quarrel with Andrew — one a lot worse than the one they had patched up a few days ago.

"I want to see how fast I can get up the hill with this bike," he said. "I'll meet you at the tourist lookout at the top of the Escarpment. Okay?"

"Sure," Andrew said cheerfully. "Hope you don't mind a bit of a wait while I plod up."

Tom got on his bike and began pedalling hard. The effort of the ride up the hill, the coolness of the breeze, made him feel better. Being able to ride all the way up with his new bike helped too.

The gravel in the lookout parking lot sparkled in the sun, and the sky behind it was a clear summer blue. As Tom gazed out over the countryside below, he began to relax. Things weren't unbearable, he decided, so long as he could have this view of his home.

The house glimmered white in the sunlight, amid the deep mid-summer green of the orchards. Occasionally the breeze carried up the sounds of trucks on the highway more than three kilometres away, but the distance gave the sounds a pleasant vagueness. Everything he cared about lay spread out before him.

The sound of footsteps crunching over the gravel made him turn around. It was Andrew. His face was red and perspiration stood out in beads on his forehead. "It's nice up here," he remarked.

"Yeah," Tom answered with contentment. "When you're rested up, let's get on to the gorge, though. The sun's hot."

They went slowly along the top of the Escarpment, not bothering to talk. At the mill a bar had been drawn across the driveway and a *closed* sign was stuck in one of the windows.

"We'll have to watch out for the runoff," Andrew said.

Tom nodded his head and looked the other way. Andrew looked at him for a moment, then shrugged his shoulders and led the way down the lane towards the path into the gorge.

They spent the rest of the morning wandering separately. Tom hiked farther down the gorge than he had ever been before, examining plants as he went and keeping an eye out for rock faces that might interest Andrew. So far his friend hadn't had too much luck in his search for unusual fossils.

In the quiet stillness of the gorge, green-shaded and cool, Tom stood and gazed at the land around him. It felt good. He wondered, as he often did in the wildness of the gorge, how the Indians had felt, surrounded always by this kind of peace.

Unconsciously he tried dancing a few steps, hop-footed, bending and turning as if with the wind. Then he stopped. No, he wasn't an Indian. He was just Tom Kirby, Chicken Man of the Escarpment.

The sense of elation trickled away. There was nothing grand and mysterious about the gorge any longer. Just trees and a stream and a bunch of rocks. Heavily he headed back towards the waterfall and the Black Tunnel. It must be long past lunch time and Andrew had the food.

When Tom reached the basin of the falls, he couldn't see Andrew anywhere. His eyes searched the trees and the rock faces, but still he couldn't see him.

"Hey, Andrew!" he yelled.

Suddenly he saw his friend's head pop out of the bushes near the lookout rock.

"Up here, Tom! I think I may have found some-thing!"

"Coming," Tom shouted as he headed for the path leading behind the waterfall. It must be really some-thing, he thought. Andrew sounded excited.

He made his way up the hidden path quickly, so quickly that he was panting for breath by the time he found Andrew crouching near some bushes.

"Look at this, Tom."

All around were loose chips of stone, with one large piece in the centre. Even Tom's untrained eyes could see the clarity of the fossil embedded on the stone. The impressions of three creatures shaped like stubby-armed starfish showed sharply under the bright light of the sun.

"Wow, that's a good one," Tom said, hoping that it

was indeed as good as it looked to him.

"It's a perfect specimen," Andrew said, his voice quick and high with excitement. "Absolutely perfect. I don't know what kind of fish these are, or the plant either. But just look at them. You can see everything!"

The starfish were only slightly larger than a twenty-five-cent piece, but the details were perfect — the surface looked granulated, with a raised bump in the centre. One of the starfish appeared to be flipped over, but Tom was not sure. There was also the clear imprint of a plant frond.

"I'll have to check in my book," Andrew went on, his eyes glinting with excitement. "I brought it today. Must have been predestined, eh? I left the knapsack down in the gorge by the first tunnel."

Tom grinned. Andrew's usually precise speech had become as garbled as his own normally was. "Want any help?" he asked as Andrew started down the path, the fossil cradled tenderly in the crook of one arm.

"No, it's okay," Andrew said distractedly. When he turned to answer, Tom could see the rapid blinking of his eyes, the signal that his mind was racing.

Comfortably Tom stretched out on top of the sun-warmed lookout rock. His mind drowsed with the warmth as through half-closed eyes he watched Andrew scramble down the slope. It would be nice if the fossil turned out to be rare. After all his work in the gorge, Andrew deserved it.

Tom's eyes strayed to the black gash of the Tunnel mouth in the rock of the cliff. He felt his stomach tense. Then he let out a deep breath and tried to relax. There was no point in getting worked up again. He had finally accepted it. He was every bit the chicken that Billy and the others said he was.

He would not challenge the Black Tunnel again. He could not bear that fear again. He would not hand himself over to the slow, dripping, squeezing terror again. Never again. It was better to be a chicken.

For a long time Tom lay still, feeling the wetness drip from his eyes and down his cheeks. It didn't matter if he was a crybaby as well as a chicken. It just didn't matter.

A shout from the gorge interrupted Tom's thoughts. Slowly he lifted his head and looked down. Andrew was sitting on a rock near the Black Tunnel, holding a book and his fossil. But he wasn't the one who had shouted.

It was Billy. Billy and the Cobras, converging around Andrew, shouting and snickering.

Tom gritted his teeth. Maybe he should go down there and give Andrew a hand. But then he remembered Billy's last words to him. The gorge would be a perfect ambush.

His mind hammered at the problem. He was the one Billy wanted to get. Maybe they would hassle Andrew, but Tom doubted they would really hurt him. No, it was better to lie low and wait for them to get bored and go away. Andrew wouldn't squeal.

With narrowed eyes, he watched the boys in the gorge below. For a while they circled Andrew, trying to scare him. Tom could imagine what his friend was saying to them — probably something about infantile behaviour. It must be something good, because even Billy was glaring helplessly at him.

Tom went over in his mind every possible way to get Billy alone for a fight. He realized very clearly now that the only way to manage Billy's hatred was to scare him — scare him so badly that he would never again try to get back at Tom and Andrew. But not now. Not when he had the other boys stirred up for a fight.

Suddenly Skinner darted forward and grabbed the fossil from Andrew's hands. Tom sat up on the rock and narrowed his eyes grimly. Cobras or not, he'd have to go down. The fossil was too important to Andrew to let those goofs play with it.

Andrew sat stock still for a moment; then he exploded into action. Tom could see his arms and legs flailing wildly as he smashed Billy in the stomach. The other boys backed off and Skinner ran, clutching the fossil.

"Bring that back!" Tom heard Andrew yell. Then his friend became tangled in himself and crashed to the ground. Skinner had run as far as the small tunnel gouged high in the cliff. He stopped and looked around frantically, panic-stricken by Andrew's sudden explosion.

"Throw it up!" screamed Billy. "Into the tunnel!"

"No!" shouted Andrew, scrambling desperately for Skinner.

Skinner hesitated a second, aimed, then threw. It was a perfect shot. The water splashed over the edge of the ledge as the fossil fell into the little pool in front of the tunnel.

Tom lay low on the rock again, watching bitterly. So the fossil now lay beside his jack-knife. But Andrew wouldn't mind going into the Black Tunnel for it. For a moment Tom almost hated him.

Andrew shouted wildly, pushed Billy roughly out of his way and ran awkwardly towards the mouth of the Black Tunnel. The Cobras ran after him, hooting and shouting derisively.

Tom began to get a queer, uneasy feeling. Something was wrong. Something — but what?

Without thinking, he stood up on the rock to get a better view as Andrew disappeared into the cold, dripping mouth of the Tunnel.

The Tunnel!

Then Tom remembered. He remembered Mr. Piers's warning. At two o'clock the water from the reservoir would pour through the Black Tunnel, sweeping away everything it caught. Quickly Tom looked at his watch.

14
Trapped!

"Andrew!" Tom screamed from the rock above. "Wait! The water!" But his friend had already disappeared into the Tunnel.

One of the boys would have to get him out. Frantically Tom started down the rough path. He slipped and skidded over some rocks, but it didn't matter. He had to get them to save Andrew.

The Cobras had seen him now, but Tom didn't care. Recklessly he rushed over the slippery rocks behind the waterfall. He heard the roar of the water. That was what the runoff would be like — a huge, insane, funnelled waterfall, snatching, suffocating and smashing Andrew against the rocks.

Tom's foot slipped and he stumbled. Desperately he clutched at some rock outcroppings and steadied himself. Then he clambered on. His heart was knocking against his ribs and he could barely breathe by the time he reached the Cobras sprawling beside the Tunnel mouth.

"Why, look who's here!" said Billy, a cruel smile spreading across his face.

"It's Chicken Man!" sang out Skinner. They began a chorus of "Buck-cluck-cluck!"

Tom clenched his fists. He couldn't believe that this was all they were thinking about.

"Remember what I told you, Chick — " Billy began.

"Shut up!" Tom shouted. "Listen to me! They're sending the reservoir water through here at two o'clock. Andrew will be killed! It's" — he looked at his watch — "it's eight minutes to two. He'll be killed! One of you has to go after him!"

Tom looked at them desperately. They knew about the power of the runoff. Even Billy's face had whitened.

"We'd better get out of here!" the Cobra's president said fearfully.

"Out of here!" Tom repeated, dazed. "We can get out of the way, but what about Andrew?" His voice cracked on his friend's name. "Billy, you're the big shot. You've got to save him!"

"Me?" Billy barked, backing off. "Forget it! I'm not going in there! Not for that creep. I could get killed too!"

"But, Billy." Mike spoke up suddenly, his voice quivering, "there's time. Remember, you did it in five minutes. You know the short cut through. He might get killed by himself. You've got to do something!"

Tom bit his lip. The Cobras looked expectantly at

their leader.

"No way," Billy said with a breathless attempt at a laugh. "Andrew can make it on his own. I'm not risking myself for him. You can go, Chicken Man, if you think it's that bad. But not me, man! Right, Cobras?"

The others looked at him in silent horror.

"Well?" Billy yelled.

"Yeah, sure," Skinner giggled nervously.

"I can't go — " Tom said almost in a whisper. He remembered the fear, the squeezing panic. He would run and let Andrew die.

"There's a short cut on the left, just inside," Mike said suddenly. "If you run your hand along the wall you'll feel the hole. You have to feel it. It's too dark to see. I — I don't think I could make it," he said in a strange, horrified voice.

Tom looked at the other boys, shifting nervously in a semicircle around Billy and himself. Billy shoved his hands into his pockets and glared at Tom.

"He's *your* friend, Chicken Man." His voice sounded odd. The others said nothing.

Tom looked around him. He felt the seconds tick off.

"You won't do anything!" he screamed at them. "You stinking bastards!"

Then he ran towards the Tunnel mouth. Wildly he plunged towards the darkness. The cold draught brushed his cheeks and bare arms. He stumbled and fell into the murky water inside the mouth.

"It's too late," Mike yelled from the entrance. "Tom, you'll both get killed."

Tom stared back in panic. He thought of Andrew's gangly legs. If he made it to the ledge on time, there was room to get back from the water. But Andrew's clumsy hands and feet could never hold on alone if the water rushed around him.

Tom scrambled to his feet and ran blindly forward—into the cruel, waiting mouth.

"Left-hand side," he gasped out. He gritted his teeth and forced his hand along the slime-covered wall as he pushed through the dark.

"Andrew!" Tom screamed. "The runoff! Come back!"

Echoes swirled around him and suddenly his trailing hand lost the feel of the wall. He shut his eyes. No! He couldn't bear the sweating blackness.

Carefully he forced himself to feel the sides of the wall. There was a narrow opening. Narrow waiting blackness. Panic screamed through Tom's mind. Not that little hole!

"No!" he screamed.

But Andrew . . . he had to go through and find him.

"Oh, God!" Tom sobbed as he pushed himself through the hole. Slime covered his shoulders and hair, but the passage widened.

He ran on, stumbling and falling twice as terror froze his legs. But he had to go on.

"Andrew!" he shouted again. "The runoff!"

The echoes swirled back, cold and mocking.

Suddenly he heard Andrew's voice. "Tom! I've got to get the fossil. It's rare. It's really rare."

Tom could hear him splashing and falling through the water ahead. The sounds grew louder as Tom thrust himself forward. He forced each foot ahead, slipping drunkenly on the mud-covered floor. He tripped on an old, rusted piece of iron rail submerged in the water and almost fell again.

Then he realized that the water was deep enough to touch his elbows. For a moment he didn't move. Far off, deep within the bowels of the Escarpment, he could hear a rumbling and a gurgling.

The water! They had opened some of the valves!

"A little at a time," Mr. Piers had said. How long before it all came?

Tom sobbed and forced himself on. He ran desperately, smashing into the rough, wet walls.

Finally the darkness lightened to a gloomy grey. The end was near! But the water was swirling wildly, trying to knock him over and carry him along.

Andrew was clinging to the side of the tunnel entrance, trying to keep his balance in the streaming water. He clutched the fossil under one arm.

"Tom!" he shouted, his face glistening and white with fear.

"Onto the ledge," Tom shouted back. "Wait, I'll help you!"

Somehow they edged around to the ledge, through the clutching, sucking rush of water. As each second passed, the torrent grew wilder in its insane plunge over the cliff. Tom and Andrew pressed their backs against the cliff wall, still warm from the sun, and listened to the trembling roar coming through the rocks.

Tom looked down into the little pool directly in front of the entrance. A bit to one side lay his rusted jack-knife, just as he had imagined it.

He began to lean over to grab it, when suddenly the rumbling grew to a roar. The water swelled through the mouth of the tunnel, inches from their bodies, thundering into the gorge below. There was a flicker of rusty red as the torrent engulfed the jack-knife and carried it away.

. Tom leaned back, desperately spreading one hand against the sheer wall of the cliff to steady himself and clutching Andrew's arm with the other. For a long time — an eternity — there was no sound in his ears but the frenzied roar of the water surging from the tunnel, wildly hurling itself over the cliff into the swelling stream in the gorge below.

Finally the water slowed and stopped. For a moment the boys stood bewildered, as the world suddenly returned to normal. Then, without words, they began to stumble back through the darkness.

The walk back was long. It was very long. Despite the almost total blackness, Tom could clearly see, sense and smell the sweating rock as it closed around him. He could feel its pressure squeezing. When his legs numbed, Andrew helped him until they finally emerged into the daylight.

The Cobras were still waiting by the stream when Tom and Andrew appeared. They stood still and silent, as if they were frozen. Suddenly Mike started away from the others and clambered up the hill to help them. Vaguely Tom remembered that Mike had once been his best friend.

"Are you guys all right?" Mike asked. "I — I've never seen anything like that water."

"Neither have I," Tom said slowly.

"We saved the fossil," Andrew announced with a look of joy on his tired face.

Tom looked at the other guys and his sense of distance faded a little. He thought they would laugh now — a couple of sadsacks stumbling out of a tunnel, covered with water and tunnel slime. He waited almost impatiently for their laughter.

But the Cobras bounded up the hill towards them. Only Billy stood motionless, fists clenched, glaring. Suddenly he turned on his heel and ran down the path, away from the others.

"You sure you guys are okay?" Mike asked again.

"Yeah, sure," Tom answered in surprise. "Where's Billy going?"

"Home," Skinner said with a quick giggle. "We kicked him out of the Cobras. Jeez, he turned out to be a bigger chicken than you, Tom. I mean — not that we ever really thought you were a chicken," Skinner added nervously with a scared grin. "You know Billy. He's such a jerk."

"Yeah," Tom said slowly. "Billy's a jerk, I guess."

"Tom," Mike said eagerly, "we held a meeting just now. That was terrific what you just did. I mean, you saved Andrew's life. And after all his big talk, Billy just stood there," he added scornfully. "So we kicked him out and voted you president of the Cobras. And Andrew's voted in too. I mean, he just passed the initiation."

And then Tom began to understand what had happened. There would be no laughter. He was the leader again. Billy's time was over and no one would sneer "Chicken Man" at him ever again. He looked at Andrew uncertainly, because something felt different about all this. He'd been thinking about it, desperately wanting and needing it for a year now — a whole year. They had exiled him and he had dreamed always of going back to the way things were — of getting even for the way his life had been ruined.

Andrew smiled wryly, then shrugged his shoulders.

Awkwardly he struggled to pick up his knapsack and slip it onto his back. Automatically Tom took it from him and slid it onto his own shoulders. The other guys were all talking and making plans and shouting, but the noise echoed through the trees and Tom didn't understand what they were saying.

Andrew looked at him and smiled slightly. "Well, Chicken Man," he said quietly, "looks as if you're captain of the team again."

"No," Tom said suddenly. "We still have too much to do. I mean, it's too late for me just to slip back."

"Hey, Tom," Mike said, giving him a friendly punch in the shoulder, "we've got a camping trip planned — an overnight at the conservation area. It's all set for next weekend. Won't it be great, man!"

"No," Tom said again, more firmly. He smiled at the other guys and it felt good. "I can't. You see, I've got the sale on the weekends. And besides," he said slowly, "I don't think I want to be president of the Club. I've got a lot of things on . . . so anyway, thanks."

"Yeah, but — " Skinner started to say.

But Tom just laughed and started running down the slope. The other guys couldn't catch up to him, and Andrew would know where to find him later.

For the first time in his life, Tom knew that he was free.